NO. 4
WINTER 2024

MIDSUMMER DREAM HOUSE
LITERARY & ARTS MAGAZINE

CALIFORNIA

Midsummer Dream House
San Diego, California
United States

Cover Photography
by Ashley Kaplan

Paperback ISBN: 979-8-9993991-6-8
Print ISSN: 3064-7819
Printed in the United States

midsummer dream house

Editor-in-Chief
Emma Grey Rose

Editor
George du Bois

Reader
Melinda Snyder

CONTENTS ↗

POETRY

B.A. O'CONNELL
Muscle Memory / 1
MATTHEW FREEMAN
Please, Understand / 2
MAUREEN MARTINEZ.
Candy-coated Cliff Houses in Morning / 3
JONATHAN CHIBUIKE UKAH
Mushrooming with My Mother / 4
JULIA LUDEWIG
Leaf-taking / 6
LEWIS LEICHER
Epithalamion / 7
STEPHEN BARILE
On *Verrue* Avenue / 8
GERARD SARNAT
Farewell My Soul's Delight? [iii]: / 10
i.tanka
ii.their concussed ass petite as piece of lettuce
iii.stages of wo/man
STEPHEN GRANT
Chronic Conditions / 11
STARRY KRUEGER
Siren Song / 12
The Hammer / 13
The Key / 14
NATASHA N. DEONARAIN
dream study 1 : grief / 15
in remembrance / 16
dream study 2 : hope / 17
BENJAMIN FRANDSEN
Moonface / 18
Dear Prison / 19

FICTION

ROSHAN MOAZED
Dream Thought / 21
ERICA HOFFMEISTER
Superstar Video / 23
PHILLIP A. LEAVENWORTH
The Museum of Alternate Worlds / 31
E.P. LANDE
The Restaurateur / 37
C.M. VINCENT
The Pyramid Scheme / 49

ART

EDWARD MICHAEL SUPRANOWICZ
Haunted by the Rustle of Wings / i
Against the Wall / vi
Chat / 78
ASHLEY KAPLAN
Out of this World / iv, 76

BIOGRAPHIES / 70

B.A. O'CONNELL

MUSCLE MEMORY

It's like this, I'm fourteen and at the bottom
of the pool waiting to drown—
but, of course—

I don't drown.

Except, what if I did?
And I am ghost, spectating my own life—
my lungs already dead,
my hands foreign instruments.

It is all just sparkling, sparkling water
in my eyes, my nose, my mouth—
I've never really learned how not to drown.

MATTHEW FREEMAN

PLEASE, UNDERSTAND

We want to be seen
but we're also really proud of the fact
that we feel like
no one can see us.

Maybe the problem is we think too highly
of ourselves, even as
bugs crowd our floor, we have to barricade
our door against our own
sleepwalking, everything
we own was given to us freely, and on top
of that we're about two checks away
from sleeping on someone's couch.

"You think
the world revolves around you,"
said Red.
"We don't actually enjoy it," we said.
We're in analysis now
to figure out if that's true.

Maybe if we sidled up nicely
to Paranoia
in our parents' bedroom
they'd have mercy on us.
P.S. our parents' bedroom is upstairs.

MAUREEN MARTINEZ

CANDY-COATED CLIFF HOUSES IN MORNING

Picturesque Portofino in June:
Chiclet cliff houses in crayon box colors-
    river salmon, saffron yellow, dusty rose.

Shuttered villa eyes slow to open
in the misty morning, espresso cups
clacking, shops rolling
    out their racks

of trendy Boho tops & bags
onto the salty cobbled square,
as breathless tourists
    pour

off boats frantic to capture
the waking port
unfurling like a white
    lotus.

JONATHAN CHIBUIKE UKAH

MUSHROOMING WITH MY MOTHER

The moon's invitation landed on my thighs
when my mother asked me with a face like flowers
to accompany her into the quiet bush.
My mother's body turned into a miracle mirror,
a globe of a glass, the reflections of the sun,
through which I saw her thousand images,
Throughout the running years of her life,
the threads of trials and tribulations of my family;
my father dashing home like an escaping criminal
trickles of sweat percolated on his forehead,
with knife slashes across his bloody back,
as though he fell on the tapestry of broken bottles;
the soldiers arresting my father to join the army,
my sisters wearing rag day dresses to church,
clanging their bangles and bracelets at passers-by.
We earned enough sympathy to purchase some rice.
When the war happened, we returned to the village
where, every day, my uncle's wife punished my mother
with words like knives that sliced her heart.

My mother led the way into the burning bush,
bushwhacking through the cluster of soggy leaves,
trees dripping with water and broken branches,
the wind whistled in our ears under the stars,
the sun withdrew before the light broke up
and the quiet spirit of the night took over.
Silence was an intrigue to darkness
while the night brought out an umbrella
to cover the marks and spurs of our feet
as we waded deeper into the forest
until we reached where the wind wept or whispered.
I didn't know when the mushrooms appeared,
wearing a large, wide white overhang
and blocking our way like silences in the wind.

We began to pick them like sunlit flowers,
or sparkling diamonds from the farm rubble,
or pearls under the rays of the midnight moon.
The air was strong like a stone; the wind was soft,
but the mushrooms felt like silk in the wind.

My mother worked away like a distant fairy,
her body hung over the star-lit beings like a canopy,
her eyes closed though darkness enveloped us,
and I knew she could see better without eyes.
How she manoeuvred her way through the forest
was a mystery that took all my life to dissolve,
working with her eyes closed and lips folded,
even as darkness moved further and further in,
sweeping aside the rays of cricket lights
and the shadows of water drops percolated on the grass.
She picked and picked, her hands teased the caps
of multitudinous mushrooms musing in the midnight,
and plugged out the intercepting shrubs and thistles
as though she shoved a child from a mound of ruin.
I watched her as the light through the crevices of the night,
fondled her face, caressed her body, kissed her brows
without lulling her to sleep or the weaknesses of the body
as though she had sacrificed her body to the time
when her family had nothing to eat except mushrooms.

JULIA LUDEWIG

LEAF-TAKING

The journey should have led to moister ground
and lucky seedlings (see the yellow sail?),
but now, the sailors come to rest in palms,
all crackling tension, courtesy of drought.

So do we meet, the leaves and I, a tête-a-twig,
on June-hot pavement. Four leaves, a scratchy
introduction as they rustle up the road, I stop
and find the tumblers at my feet.

I bend my own parched torso over them and raise
the flyweight to the squinting of my eyes:
all leaves arrested in a closing gesture, a snapshot
of a cramping hearts' quartet.

It takes the slender, tawny bract to know its name,
the twins of embryonic fruits subtended.
I stare into the wind to trace the tree, but fail:
too far from home and still in transit.

My nosey nose gets tickled by the leaves
who have long lost their famous smell,
no honey fragrance, tea, no sticky goodness,
just warmth, and very faint, a whiff of smoke.

The taste is strong, instead, a crunchy bitter,
glucose ghosts with asphalt and bitumen.
How long, I wonder, does my spittle need to dry,
To send the leaves where they were headed
      to trash bags,
      bug mouths,
       or yet another linden lover.

EPITHALAMION

You're my wife and I'm your husband, finally.

We were boyfriend and girlfriend as seniors in college,
over 40 years ago, then "more than friends" and then
long-distance pen pals who saw each other in person
occasionally through our 20s. A decade of little contact
followed (we were in difficult marriages, and you had kids),
then we were lovers again, then partners and best friends,
and now we're hitched. Normally, I'm not one for labels,
but the variety of our connections, over the years,
made me want to try to categorize and name them.

Now we expect to grow old together, and mock argue
about who'll kick the bucket first: you say you, I say me,
and we joke about what the other will do when they're "free."
I think maybe, from the start, I've never really been free
of you and never will be (unless, as I've said, I die first).

We are dissimilar in so many ways: our temperaments,
our personalities, our ways of speaking, but there was
and still is an ease of understanding, an ease of feeling,
that made and makes loving you as natural as breathing.

We wrote poems to each other when we were younger
and here I am, at it again. I promise there's no agenda,
no hidden plan to push you to put pen to paper. I'm just
making sure you get it in writing that I am yours, forever.

STEPHEN BARILE

ON VERRUE AVENUE

A Tuesday night,
Riding my bike home,
North on 10th Street
To *Verrue* Avenue.
Byways empty tonight,
Everyone is home at 8 P.M.,
No traffic to contend with.
In front of the television set,
You could tell, blue light
Radiates from the windows

On *Mono* or *Balch* Avenues.
At *Verrue*, a turn by instinct
And desire. A small park, left
That no one ever speaks of
And may not have a name;
An acre and a half, and a pump.
On the East *Tulare* right-of-way,
Freight trains hauled fruit
Down the middle of the street,
Turned north toward *McKenzie*.

Across from modest houses
On East *Verrue* Avenue,
Between 10th, and 11th,
Station 4, a city water-well
With neat flower beds
Of blooming red perennials.
Among the trees, magnolias, ash,
A Valley oak, a few willows,
Three palms, and a pine.
Well-irrigated and deftly pruned.

Groomed bushes, manicured trails,

Grass regularly mowed.
A pine tree, original landscaping
When the city grew east this way.
In the interior of the park,
A well-established Magnolia tree.
Old, thickly limbed, neatly-trimmed,
A lemony fragrance in the air.
Providing abundant shade
For lovers seeking solitude.

Third house from the corner,
The two-story white one,
That's where Donna C. lived.
I rode by there often
Hoping to see her.
Tonight, under the porch-light,
She might wave as I glide by.

FAREWELL MY SOUL'S DELIGHT? [iii]

i.tanka

no old pigeonholes:
fluidity's new brilliant
frame — container holds
continuum gender mix
match -- times change/ mistypes uncaged!

ii.their concussed ass petite as piece of lettuce

sizing us up before a code switch
oy kinda dude who walks on knuckles
Boy have I got something for you!
then bludgeoned twerker jerk to death.

back to strip mall strip-club grind
where sex is sold so fast johns do not
bother take off socks unless horn
dog goes to next door hour-rate motel.

there feckless fucks must pay overtime.

iii.stages of wo/man

going steady
steadier going
unsteady, gone

STEPHEN GRANT

CHRONIC CONDITIONS

Overflowing waste, signs of indolence and spiritual torpor.
As the curtain descends, the wall shadows turn opalescent. They
darken into a void, a cool chiaroscuro, a crescent cream moon
in a coral blue sky, never to be seen again. At least in this lifetime.
Atmospheric particulate crowds my space. I've lost my way,
hearing the screen door screech into urban floss, nine floors up.
Canyon streets lined with colored flags, cheering the unknown,
the emptiness. Neural pathways abound, running amok, highlighting
my litmus test of feeling. Drip-dropping acid into a velvet base,
there's no time for second-guessing. Sensing the echoes from the water
droplets, the crystal shards, I am fiercely indignant at the disruption
of my melancholy. As found in the liturgy, the fear of death perturbs
me. And not for the first time, I feel the Sirens calling. But it's only
a drill, a test, and hardly worth the heed. Invisible molecules coalesce,
cresting in time. They cause chaotic reflection. So, I fill mesh bags
with useless contemplation, try to suss out the meaning of a pumpkin
sitting on my table in a still-life pose, like a Dutch master's skull next
to an ancient globe. *Memento mori.* Chaos beckons, with its saturnine
air. As it's time to end, lend me a thought and put some oomph into it.
Abstraction comes at a price, and I was always a sucker for red.

SIREN SONG

Mama walked into the water.
She was never to return.
Did she have stones inside her pock-
ets or a tail below her waist?
No matter what her reasons Mama left
without a trace.

Daddy looked for answers at the bot-
toms of his bottles.
The children liked to daydream,
liked to daydream,
just like Mama did.

The son would experiment with the
sounds of his father's empty bottles.
And the rhythms of the tools in his
father's shop.
The daughter found mother's books of
poetry and memorized every word.

Their father said this noise meant
nothing
And he would throw all of his anger
and fear at his family.

Fear of failure, fear of loss, fear of
loneliness.

And the children would cling to each
other and cry.

They recognized their mother's face in
the wood.
Their tears seeped into her grains.
That salt water can't be washed away.

Tears of failure, tears of loss, tears of
loneliness.

While they held the boat,
they would listen to the sounds of their
father in his woodshop.

The daughter cringed at the sound.
She would think of her mother's poet-
ry and imagine she was some place
peaceful and still.

Her brother found the rhythm of the
hammer oddly comforting.
Like the waves crashing on the shore.
He felt compelled to carry these
rhythms with him.
So he became a drummer.

THE HAMMER

One daughter searching swam down with the sun
The other waiting drums and drinks and dreams
The hammer will not rest 'til its work is done

Mermaids are accused of mischief and schemes
They protect themselves against betrayal
Grief reverberates within siren's screams

Messages in bottles are mermaids' mail
The cork keeps the ink from washing to sea
To avoid mermaids' bite catch her by tail

A lost child hopes the ocean will hear her plea
She puts her faith in a stranger's drumming
Father's secrets are under lock and key

The drunk insists on singing and humming
She hopes to conjure women in the deep
The women were lured by distant drumming

The child has nightmares when she goes to sleep
One daughter searching swam down with the sun
Old family secrets are hard to keep
The hammer won't rest til its work is done

THE KEY

The key
that you burn
Has been passed down for genera-
tions.
We have always known,
The lock stretching from our throats
through our wombs,
To the core of the earth

Is alive.

Grounding rod
Snake
Divining rod
Serpent

To keep us safe
from those
Who would burn it
We made a key
Forged in the fire of truth
So those who sought to extinguish us
Wouldn't see the power we held.

But dear one,
The key was never for them.
It was our secret
So we could pass the fire
On to you.

We passed it on in a million ways
The crackle of the pot
Sizzling garlic and onions

The strength of our biceps
Carrying babies and kneading fresh
dough
Sparks flying from our cigarettes
Telling it like it is

Do not mistake the key
We did not want to lock our fire in
We wanted to protect it
So we could pass it on to you.

Now you burn the key.
We watch it melt.
Golden ashes fill the air
We laugh and clap as we watch it
transform.

Grounding rod
Snake
Divining rod
Serpent

Stay unlocked, child.

We are here now.
Arms outstretched
Heads thrown back
Teeth bared and joyful
Unafraid
We will protect you now.

Stay unlocked.
We dance around your fire.

DREAM STUDY 1 : GRIEF

a sun pasted with haste onto a cornflower-blue tissue paper sky,
its edges unfurled and dripping with glue, torn patches
where white cotton bulges through, the gouged cardboard
ground with a few dusty pebbles and unfinished roads
leading to endless vanishing points—

someone took a can of spray paint and graffitied the land and
sky as if contiguous like stretched hide across time—

the putrefied smell of breath suspended in thick caves,
splotched with feather, fur and dead skin—

in the foreground, a crushed blue and silver can of michelob,
crumpled mcdonalds wrappers, a half-box of musty, dried
fries, a garish footprint next to cigarette butts, ash and tire
tread skid marks racing away from a place where even grief
won't stay—

NATASHA N. DEONARAIN

IN REMEMBRANCE

In the sedated aftermath of a restless Nyquil™ night,
sound-slapped half-awake by motors ripping up the day,
the anxious arms of the sun disarrayed and I'm not sure
if it was just a dream—I'm trying to remember what it was
that grafted this silence between us, an ever-expanding
track of dysesthesia where nerve connections no longer
cross, the anaesthesia of our relationship built upon
something that happened sometime when, with a few
characters we knew from a play I paid a high price to watch
and I'm trying to remember the plot that lead to such
volcanic eruptions, tectonic faults and lava that flowed
between us and then cooled into Pompeiian shapes I brush
past as if in a vault, and I'm trying to remember the way
it used to be with us before that time, but all I come up with
is sun-kissed air filled with aromas of steak au poivre,
gratin Dauphinois and garlic-buttered asparagus tips on a
white tablecloth, garden filled with Peace lilies, hydrangea
and clematis vines, the laughter and clink of our glasses
overflowing with a carefully chosen, finely-aged wine—

DREAM STUDY 2 : HOPE

scintillating beach and effervescent sea fringed with grass-
bearded sand banks, coiffed by trees done in acrylic paint
dripped and smeared as the ground reshapes itself when tilted
in all directions to recolor this place—

a disco-ball sun spins in front of a confetti night sky that then
breaks into a kaleidoscope dawn, birds drawn like delicate
black mustaches that dip and swoop against the mercurial
glare as airplanes are shot through air like silver bullets from
a smoking gun—

in the bottom right corner, a pair of glittering five-inch ruby
red pumps perched there waiting for feet to wear, a silk dress
on a hanger pulling away from the canvas sheet, its left
shoulder half in 3-D and rippling length pooling to the floor
like a red wave, a suspended tube of crimson lipstick poised
to paint a pair of lush lips that have yet to appear, and at the
horizon's edge on the left, a blushing blue sky that bleeds
into whirlpools and spills over the side—

MOONFACE

My childhood self looked down at me
  from deep in the full moon's face.
His eyes did not remember me,
  for these eyes took their place.
He squinted his eyes and frowned and said,
  "You looked like a boy I knew.
Just then when you titled up your head,
  I saw my light in you—
a ghostly and familiar light
  that chilled my moonlight spine.
For if you were the boy who once took flight,
  this perch would not be mine."
"Took flight?" quivered I, with moonstruck eye,
  "How flew? And flew where to?"
"To the land of the grown-up jaded lies,
where there is no wonder if their eyes,
  no play and just to-do."
"Can I...can he...can we come back?"
  And how will we find our way?"
"When worldly eyes find light they lack,
  the blackness turns to day."
Then looking down, I saw a man—a stranger in my shoes.
  He looked at me through moonlit skies,
  my moonface did not recognize,
  and the man with sad, unboyish eyes
dissolved in jaded hues.

BENJAMIN FRANDSEN

"DEAR PRISON"

Dear Prison,
>I'm sorry
>to have to do this
>on paper

But the truth is,
>in eighteen years,
>you've only spoken to me
>in the clinking of cruel chains,
>the strangled cry of hope,
>the finality
>of metal doors clanging shut.

So a letter seems as fitting a way as any
>to let you know
>it's over.

After losing myself
>and then finding myself
>in every self-help on the shelf,
>I can say with certainty:

It's not me,
>it's you.

You did your best
>to stamp out my crackling flame,
>beastify my humanity,
>make me hate other colors—
>black, brown, yellow
>and green.

But it didn't take:
>I love my other-colored brothers;
>I love my family and friends
>more than ever.

I even love you
>in a he-don't-know-no-better,
>maybe-someday kind of way.

In a few days, when I wave goodbye

"DEAR PRISON"

and punctuate "life sentence"
with my period of lifelong freedom,
don't cry.
I'll be back
for my many-colored brothers in blue—
to help them shake you,
cut the ties that bind them.
dissolve the prisons in their minds.
After all, if our minds are free,
you are nothing but a construct of darkness,
and if you are dragged out
into the light,
you too will someday
be dissolved.

ROSHAN MOAZED

DREAM THOUGHT

It was a dream where I saw it, an eggshell cradling a thought, placed gingerly behind a semicolon; huddling close to its parent thought, too shy to peck its way into the light. So I moved towards the eggshell, spherical and shinning copper like a penny in a light beam of sunrise, and began to unpeel it as though it were boiled, flaking the shell off in pieces with my fingernails, feeling the dull-sharp ridges wedge between the skin of my thumb and nailbed, unwrapping a present so carefully packaged I was almost fearful to touch it, as though it might disintegrate into dust in the clasp of my calloused palms, far more austere than an eggshell housing a thought, whatever it was, hiding anxiously behind the semicolon as slowly it unveiled. I worked for hours at this, not wanting to scare the thought away, not wanting it to run into a golden puddle of egg yolk, surrounded by clear slime and flecks of white, removing pieces of shell the size of specks, of particles hovering in the August air of a dream, thick humid and subverting the human eye. Searching for what it cannot see.

Finally, after beads of sweat had rolled down the back of my neck and collected into one at the bottom of my spine, leaving a dark spot on my t-shirt, after the sun fell below the tree crowns and the sky had turned lavender and cool, I opened the Dream Thought at last. The eggshell lay dismantled on the stone tiles of our garden steps where I had done my work. Below us blueberry bushes turned to shadows, robins flying home with sweet berries in their beaks, honey bees retreating somberly to a place more mysterious. The thought itself was scarlet, like the side of a brick building on fire while the sun breathes in the last viable angle of the axis, before the Earth rotates a fraction more, counter a clock, and the streets are cast in a shadow. It was bumpy, like the skin of a goose that has been plucked, naked, torn from what gave it flight, what let it fly in V-shapes across a pond, murky and green in the summer, a glassy blue in January, but we were in August, now. I couldn't understand it, though it was staring at me with wide, thoughtful eyes. It was as though this eggshell baby thought, hitched to a parent thought, was too young to speak to a stranger such as myself, the parent thought said never speak to those you don't know, no matter how long they spend birthing you under the scorching sun of an August dream, no matter how carefully they unwrapped you in the lemon light of sleep.

DREAM THOUGHT

You can share your secret with no one.

This secret Dream Thought in the garden, rescued for nothing but to stare at me, thought-like, and for me to stare back, scarlet and goose-skinned, we both were, flightless, hitched to a dream, a boat drifted across a pond with emerald water, we couldn't fly in a V-shape, now, we were plucked, from waking worlds, from the sunlight, we existed in a shadow, as the honey bees flew home to a mystery and the robins flew to tree crowns, staining violet juice onto the open beaks of loved ones. Me and this odd type of chick, born featherless, born silent, born a brick illuminated in light, hitched to a parent thought that would have been a sentence of its own but for today, that told it not to share secrets, lemon light dreamscape or not.

Me and the Dream Thought sat on the stone steps and looked out at the sea of grass below us, moving in waves and crashing upon a shore of itself, at the moths beginning to bump against the lightbulb wedged where the wall of the house met the roof, a dim glow against the indigo of seven-thirty in August, in a Dream, a Thought, a mosquito rising from the shallows of night and burrowing into my thigh. It was a dream, it was August, it was an eggshell, empty, behind a semicolon in front of a parent, whispering tell your secret to no one, be silent in the wake of the sun.

SUPERSTAR VIDEO

She has small hands, rebelliously soft and feminine despite twice-daily swims in our high school's overchlorinated pool. Her delicate fingers tenderly bunch up the fishnet stockings into donuts; a rote skill leftover from nearly every girl's over-sequined, early-90s childhood dance hobby. She slips her right leg in first, toe pointed, pulls the black webbing over her skin. Repeats the same poised motion with the other to raise both legs in the air, toes nearly reaching the ceiling as she pulls the waistband up and over her torso. My mattress caves under the sudden weight of her body as she flounders back onto her stomach with dramatic breath, as if it's difficult for her to move so effortlessly through movements of womanhood. She does everything like this—pretends she doesn't know exactly how to be. Her body understands air as it does water. Something to part and separate and become.

"Are you going to wear that skirt?" she asks, hands cupping her chin.

I stand there, watching her legs swing back and forth in the air like an eggbeater. The same motion her swim coach instructed me to mimic as my body filled with lead and sank me to the bottom of the pool that summer. I never could understand gravity while shouldering the stone-weight of defiance.

"I don't know, should I?" I inspect the knee-length denim skirt I'm wearing. It looks suddenly hideous, something my mom would wear to church to hide her unshaven kneecaps.

"You're supposed to wear a miniskirt with fishnets," she explains, rolling over and off my bed, landing on the carpet. Her toes are poking through the cheap, black webbing, tearing through. A tiny constellation of extra holes stretching and conceding into their own widened pattern—but we wouldn't notice it just yet.

She marches to my tiny closet and pulls out a black Lycra skirt, an 80s relic of my mom's that I stole from the back of her closet, hanging behind her floral church dresses.

"Like this," she says simply, pulling it over her narrow hips.

"I have an idea." I fetch my pair of fabric scissors from my windowsill and kiss the blades to denim, the cool metal grazing the tops of my leg. A clandestine thrill felt in each tear of fabric, reverberating with every slice. Rip and fray, become something else entirely.

SUPERSTAR VIDEO

She helps me finish around the back, cutting right below the crease of my glutes where my thighs sprout down to the earth into unruly limbs. I wonder when my body will feel more human, less botanic. Adults are always comparing it to budding flowers, unstoppable weeds. She removes the strip of denim from its former self and tosses it onto the carpet.

"There. Perfect."

Our fishnetted skin glows hairless under patterned holes as we slip into chunky heels and strap our ankles in. Secured, abundant. This is the way girls fall in love with one another. With access to a deep-inside private girl-space, impossibly unknown by lovers, or boyfriends, or husbands.

We take turns matting our faces with cheap CoverGirl powder like my mom models for us before school dances and dot our foreheads and nose until our brightness is subdued.

"The T-Zone," I instruct, her chin in my palm. I paint her eyes with black kohl liner, my fingers stretching her lids into a smooth canvas as the colors around her pupils fetch specks of light in violent hazel sunbursts. Her hair is matted slick against the sides of her face like always, strands over-oiled from chlorine damage treatments. She smacks her lips in conclusion. We are finally ready.

In my flimsy, discolored full-length mirror we examine ourselves. Re-gloss our lips and suck in our organs, spinning and stretching and inspecting every inch of self.

"We look like hookers," I say, giggling at how the word settles at the downturns of my mouth.

"Success," she smiles, her arm around my bare shoulder.

It was her idea to dress up for our Friday afternoon ritual walk to the video store. We can rent anything we wanted if we looked old enough, no questions asked, she explained. All we need is the laminated turquoise membership card with the neon gold stars scattered across the logo, my phone number handwritten on the back: 765-2151, no area code. No identification needed. No parents, no rules. With enough change, enough modification, we can become anything we want to.

It's nearly two miles from my house to Superstar Video. We walk this route often. We round the curved road behind my house that lines the divide between our lives and the ones resting in hillside mini-mansions on multi-acre plots of orange groves and infinity pools. Behind the high school gated with tall chain-link fencing that's broken in sections for casual spectators to pass through and watch the baseball team practice under muscle-glistening sun. Up the street with the most stop lights in deliberate view of passerby. A quick stop at the Circle-K to share a suicide-slushie we pay with found change to trek the last few blocks down the east end of our town's seven-mile main street. And finally, across one of many empty dirt fields that speckle our small town's existence.

The last few steps of our journey are scored by whirrs of cars driven famously slow—a forgotten valley of retirees shadowed by the San Jacinto Mountains. The occasional honk or catcall a mark to carve into our collective belt of female adolescent conquest. Such naively inverse notions of conquest and conqueror at age fourteen. Tides of want and regret, not knowing which one we should gravitate towards. Things we'd eventually wedge between one another and pretend to not know why we had drifted apart. For now, we are one entity; our separation is as unimaginable as the digital revolution.

We link arms as our inadequate shoes hit loose, desert earth, crossing the threshold where the sidewalk ends. In our wobbly heels, we dodge the concrete debris drizzled across the dirt field, the video store at last perched in view. Each stumble jolts from a panicked ankle, vibrating up our bones and to our teeth. We laugh, catching each other's bodies as we traverse the sea of dust and brush and freedom.

A goathead lodges into the webbing of my fishnets and catches itself between my toe's gaps. I buckle, landing on my chest and hands, arms turkeyed out, drawing my shoulder blades into my spine.

"Are you okay?" she crouches, her hand grasping my elbow. I remove the goathead from my toe, its sting burning the pad of my foot. "You're covered in them now," she laments, lifting me to my feet.

In the field, she squats to pick each individual goathead from my stockings, my legs exposed, the lasting itch that always remains from the sticker's thorns burning my skin like fire ants' stings. There are dozens stuck in my stockings, threatening a breach in the arrowslits of the webbing. Her fingers move on course, delicate archers of my defense.

With her low against my legs, I stand tall and watch as a sedan slows, pulling over against the curb beside us. The window meters down as someone inside cranks it by hand.

"What are you girls doin'? Everything OK?" A man's voice calls from inside the car, a shadow of anonymity.

SUPERSTAR VIDEO

She stands up immediately, turns and thrusts up a stiff middle finger without hesitation. Her seasoned muscles tighten, shoulders as broad as the valley horizon, as she stretches her arm farther, finger higher, until the driver finally takes the hint and peels away. We're both eldest daughters, defense for another instinctually rises violently without hesitation. She's thirteen months older than me, the hierarchy innate. I can never do the same for myself.

"Asshole," she says, bending back over to brush the last of the earth from my legs. "You're good, now," she assures me.

We finish the remaining yards of our journey hand in hand, reaching the glass doors with gasping breaths. The sun us perfectly warm on the backs of our arms as we enter, the temperature of filtered light as if through a magnifying glass, zoomed in, seconds from igniting into flame.

Inside, we take stock, the harsh blow of air conditioning spiking up the hair on gooseflesh arms. Propped on the back wall's shelves of the video store are the new releases: VHS displays of clear clamshells behind each mini-movie poster cover. Things moved slowly back then—the space and time of waiting between theatrical release and VHS rentals sometimes a full year; an entire lifespan in teenaged years. Each title film had already been picked off quickly by early Friday evening; by nightfall, the lucky patrons will be nestled up on their oversized loveseats watching *American Beauty, Fight Club,* or the newest James Bond, eating popcorn from a microwaved paper bag.

"Not this section," she whispers. "Too obvious."

She leads us into the aisle of older Rated-R titles. I brush my fingers across the hard plastic cases as I follow her down the winding routes of opportunity, every film a different world to discover, a different persona to momentarily adopt. I'd follow her anywhere. I pause my step, my index finger resting on a psychedelic neon smorgasbord of images. A new dimension altogether.

"Hey," I call to her, pointing. "How about this one?"

She clunks over to remove the video from its place on the eye-level shelf. *"...Sexy, psychedelic, dementedly funny with a sensational soundtrack,"* she reads from the cover, her eyes glittering with intrigue. Her head rests on mine as she places a finger on the violent red still shot of the couple's tongues touching.

"It's 'Beverly Hills 90210' on Acid," I read the tagline mockingly, trying to understand simultaneous shame and excitement, the iron gates of adulthood's arousal and curiosity beginning to part.

All I know about on-screen sex or drugs are from the few times I left my bedroom for a snack and caught my parent's own VHS rental selections—our kitchen conveniently adjacent to the living room. At the exact moment Sharon Stone spread her legs in *Basic Instinct.* In time for the mockery of sex and obsession with virginity (and why we shouldn't apparently keep ours) as championed by *American Pie*, a movie my dad wasn't supposed to tell me he found hilarious. During the scene where Jude Law stands up from the bathtub in *The Talented Mr. Ripley* and I jumped from my seat beside my mom in the theater, heart-pounding-nervous that she saw I saw his full penis projected widescreen in front of us. It was always an accident, acknowledging sex on screen. Always a sharp pang of red-hot flush on the cheeks, hoping no one noticed that I noticed. I always notice.

This movie that I'm holding in my un-calloused hands feels intentional and secret. It's a neon monologue of nihilism, flashing adolescence, shouting, outright bragging about sex, sex, sex.

"Perfect," she says, satisfyingly.

We sink our shoulders down and lift our chins to summon the confidence of the actresses on the cover of our selected movie: *Nowhere*, directed by Gregg Araki.

On unsteady doe legs, we present the tape to the clerk. It is the first of many tests. What else can we get away with in these costumed bodies?

Barely older than us, yet an entire generation ahead of us, the clerk doesn't even raise his eyes to see our spaghetti-strapped shoulders, the glitter we rolled onto our decollates that smell like fruited hand sanitizer. "It's due in 5 days," he says simply, sliding the VHS over the demagnetizing strip and placing it with receipt on the backside of the counter to be collected on our way out.

We follow our exit route swiftly, our eyes wide, attempting to hide our deep parts spiked with a sudden dopamine rush. I grab the VHS and we bolt out the door to release a flurry of breath and laughter, limbs tied together in victory. We tramp the long back way home as the sun sets behind our brown hills, a momentary realization of something temporary.

In my bedroom, I push the VHS tape into my white combo TV/VCR, gears grinding the tape to *play.* For a moment, the ribbon twists around the threading posts, relaying a scratchy feed on the tiny, curved screen. I eject the tape, hand it to my best friend to untwist and rethread the ribbon while I retrieve the flathead screwdriver that I keep beside it for times like this. I shove my tool into door-flap and wiggle it around a bit, just like the owner of Gary's TV & VCR Repair showed me. Click the movie back into place and let it play.

I always have my wooden desk chair up pushed against the door to prevent the inevitable sibling from intruding—they know better, know what her and I are capable of by now, the years between them and us recently expanding from a few years into a lifetime. My tiny, closet-sized bedroom becomes a portal, my twin bed that takes up most of the floorspace our transport. I stand to unscrew the lightbulb from the exposed overhead light, the thin glass mount shattered by one of my dad's drunken tantrums months ago, as the switch beside my door controls both the light and the TV simultaneously. These small movements of habit, of adaption I never noticed as a signal of our poverty. Of burden.

Such normalcy in the acceptance of inconvenience, of the broken things, the overwhelming lack-of what we consider luxury. And yet, we never miss a step. Change, alter, survive. We feel superior in our resilience, our resourcefulness required to survive this shit town. Those rich girls from school could never stand a chance in our world. That we knew for certain, keep the fact close to our chests like Kevlar.

The tiny screen exhibits a barrage of sensory response. Fast moving colors, a big star cameo in each scene. The soundtrack to end all soundtracks. There's no Googling to tell us what LSD is, what a threesome is, so we closely analyze each edgy sex-slash-drugs scene together, deconstruct the flashing neon existential disrepair that we don't realize already exists within our own bodies. We enter that moment as teenagers and will leave as creatures of untamed knowledge. Bonded in messy, confusing growth within eighty-two minutes.

But the actors on the screen aren't us, despite claiming to be. They're of the generation older, like the video store clerk: the disaffected Gen-X. Those all-important years distorting how linear our timelines will always feel. We look to the twenty-something actors playing who were supposed to be us high school girls: lonely, sex-driven, drug-induced, depressed. Leading us through a kind of life that will die before we even approach it. Beautiful, confused, doomed.

Are we doomed, yet? Can we possibly know how close we are to the end of everything, longing for destruction of a world we'd one day miss fondly? As elder millennials, our world is still closed in, protected. That suburban hell, something we will at some point in midlife, crave the safety of. Our futures displayed on screen, promising something it will never provide.

———

Superstar Video will have eventually outlasted Y2K, 9/11, the recession, and my best friend and I's close friendship. Nearly twenty years later, I'll come across a Facebook post announcing of its final closure. I'll be living hundreds of miles away, three lifetimes later, but I'll feel the tangible, thick plastic of my membership card between the pads of my fingers when I learn of its end.

I'll remember vividly the smell of those Friday nights, fragrant with orange blossoms and loose dust and slurpies and palm tree breezes. I'll think of the scent of gel pens cascading over lined paper, narrating my dreams to my once-best friend about *chocolate*, our secret code word for sex, named for Ryan Phillippe's brazen oral sex act in the movie that changed us. A symbolic, desperate desire to rid ourselves of innocence, not knowing how doomed we would too, in turn, become.

I'll search and search for a copy of *Nowhere* without success for years. Memories of the lost world trapped between a graveyard of clamshell VHS cases, the ribbons of film worn thin, my last owned VCR a heap of gears and motors, abandoned in disrepair.

But then, one day, I will find it.

I'll be rummaging through a used media store called Black and Read in Colorado somewhere north of the nearest suburb's skeletal remains with my husband and two young daughters. As a team, we'll be on the hunt for a cassette tape to play in our 2000 Landcruiser, with luck, a used copy of Bikini Kill for my five-year old who's wearing her vintage 90s green felt hat for the sixty-second day in a row. I'll never learn how to live in the present.

And there it will be.

Nowhere.

Anticlimactic. Blended within the sea of dusty, forgotten titles. Sitting there on a spinning wire rack marked for $7.99.

"HOLY SHIT ON EBAY THIS IS WORTH—"

My husband will give me the eyes he often does when filtering through people's trash. We don't want to signal the used video store owner's farsightedness of this precious title. He doesn't know how much this VHS is worth. No one knows its true value, anyway.

It's like Beverly 90210 on Acid...

I'll finger the cover over the tagline for the first time in twenty years, visceral, tangible, unforgotten. The smell the chlorine scent of her hair, the finger webs of her delicate hands inserting mine as she rests her head on my shoulder beneath that desert-valley sky we both escaped, but never left completely.

PHILLIP A. LEAVENWORTH

THE MUSEUM OF ALTERNATE WORLDS

Note: Entry into the Museum is free with the price of admission

Llewelyn was the 25-year-old kid being shepherded around the Museum by the Docent. Today was his first day as a volunteer for the Natural History Museum of Alternate Worlds, located not far from the rim of the Grand Canyon. The Museum is known for sapping visitors from the Grand Canyon, the Planes of Fame Museum, and the Meteor Crater. The word Alternate Worlds comes from the portmanteau for 'alternate and externalities.

The Museum uniform was a khaki shirt and khaki pants. The Docent chose the long sleeve. He remembered going to the Museum when he was about age seven. He'd ask his fiancée to marry him there. As the two men entered the Main Lobby of the Museum, Llewelyn noticed the giant statue of the founder of the Museum. A small bronze plaque at the statue's feet read 'Ulysses S. Ulysses (1876-1931)- Beloved Founder and Discoverer of Alternate Worlds.' The figure showed a man in a straightened posture holding his suit jacket lapel, with his chin held toward the future. Behind the statue, beside the Gift Shop, was an enormous pyramid that seemed to be taller than the interior of the building would allow.

"What made you want to volunteer for this place?" asked the Docent.

"I've been coming here since I was a kid. I wanted to be a part of its history," replied Llewelyn.

"Well, certainly part of someone's history. You see, this local industrialist and philanthropist founded this place. In 1929, when he founded the Museum, he leaped to his death. Though he survives the fall in some timelines, in others he never existed. Like twenty years before, he was trying to find gold, oil, or some shit. Ultimately, he kept dredging up these objects, people, and other paraphernalia with suspicious origins," said the Docent.

"Yeah, some on the University circuit say it might be caused by aliens, time slips, or the porous flaws in the simulacrum," said Llewelyn as they crossed the boundary of the Main Lobby and entered the adjacent hallway to the Staff Elevators.

A series of warning labels had been pasted around the grounds of the

THE MUSEUM OF ALTERNATE WORLDS

Museum to warn would-be adventurers from venturing too far into any of the inactive exhibits. The warning label near the Staff Elevators read: 'Your further admittance into the Museum is not recommended if you have ever ingested LSD, peyote, ayahuasca, or any other form of DMT or psychedelics.'

"So far, even the most *expert* experts can't come up with a solid answer for anything here. It just is. As for me, I'd like to keep it that way," the Docent sighed.

The Docent handed Llewelyn a copy of the Museum Map to guide him through the rest of the day's activities. Throughout the day, he'd take him through the various Halls of the Museum. On the second level, the Hall of Zoology showcased various alternate biologies of creatures from different timelines worldwide. Even alternate versions of Homo Sapiens and timelines where the dinosaurs did not go extinct.

Yet another section of the Museum held the Hall of History, the most extensive area of the Museum. It showcased items from worlds where the Nazis won World War II or the Confederacy defeated the Union during the Civil War.

"This spot is really popular with a very specific group of people," the Docent interjected as he noted the gaggle of pale-skinned, mohawked men interspersed within a larger group of bald men wearing leather.

As they continued, another exhibit was dedicated to the Man from Another Country in Another Time. The man in question claimed to the Customs officials in Japan during the 1950s that his nation of Lantea existed between what we'd call France and Spain. Ultimately, the country failed to show up on any maps despite the man's claims that his country had been around for thousands of years. Regardless of the man's death in the 1980s, his journal is still written as his fountain pen hovers above a page and constantly writes page after page. The Sanitation Department typically handled the resupply of journals for the pen.

Venturing even further, the Red Moon exhibit displayed a Soviet LK-Lander that landed on the Moon in 1968, a year earlier than the United States did in the regular timeline. A full-scale mockup of Alexei Leonov's space suit stood beside the Lander with its hand clasped firmly onto a flagpole that displayed the colors of the Soviet Union. A laminated photo of the phrase Нашамечта1 was hung under the space suit. Depending on the timeline, some hyperintelligent cosmonaut dogs had been the first to land on the Moon instead.

Not far from that display was an exhibit of the Nixon assassination. A Nixon Half-Dollar, some newspaper clippings, and images of the event blanketed a series of TVs that mimicked a storefront of the era. In that timeline, it was Richard Nixon who was assassinated in 1963 instead of JFK. That timeline ended in a nuclear war with Russia in 1973. Llewelyn looked down at the map and noticed a section on the lowest level of the Museum indicated with red stripes and the words RESTRICTED AREA, etched into the little box for the section. For whatever reason, Llewelyn felt compelled there by some outside force he could not describe or even understand fully.

"Doc, what's this spot?" asked Llewelyn, pointing at the map.

"Rook, we only have G-tier access. It's well above both our pay grades," the Docent replied.

The Restricted Area was located in the basement and was split into two sections—one for uncategorized items and the other for dangerous objects that have yet to be displayed. But the Docent decided to show Llewelyn the final section on the second level, the Hall of You, where one could view different versions of the person occupying the Hall.

"So what if I don't see myself?" asked Llewelyn.

"Rook, it could mean anything. Some say it means you don't exist there at all, or that you died long before you could come here. Either way, it's up to you if you want to see it," the Docent said in an exasperated exhale.

Nevertheless, the two men entered the Hall, not expecting anything in particular. But this was not the first rodeo for the Docent. The Hall was a nondescript room with gray walls, a large glass barrier separating an adjoining room, and a small scale-sized pad on the ground. Llewelyn walked over to the center of the room and stood on the pad.

"Give it a moment," the Docent said.

The moment seemed to last forever, but a fuzzy image coalesced into a silhouette behind the barrier in the adjoining room's pad before forming a distinct figure. This figure wore a black suit and tie, not unlike typical business attire. Save for a small badge that hung from one of his suit pockets that stated: 'Bureau of Alternate Affairs- Llewelyn Lowry- San Francisco, California.' Llewelyn exchanged looks at his Other-Self. His Alter only looked at him with disgust and stepped off the pad.

"Well, that was weird," Llewelyn said.

---

1 Russian phrase translating to "Our Dream" in English.

"Have you never been here before?" the Docent said.

The day continued. They had lunch at the Food Court, where the Docent insisted on getting ice cream, but Llewelyn was not a fan. All he could think about was the Restricted Area. He asked the Docent if he could remain after hours for a bit, and ultimately, he was allowed as long as he assisted the Sanitation Department. The Museum closed at 5 P.M. during the week and was closed on the weekends.

He swept the back of the Hall of History. Llewelyn noticed the Nixon Half-Dollar again and took it off its display. He was fascinated that there could ever be a world where JFK had lost and that Nixon would be the revered statesman, but he was not in this timeline. Absent-mindedly, he shoved it into his pocket when one of the Janitorial staff startled him as they went down the elevator with a mop and bucket.

Unfortunately, the museum staff was not known for their competency, which did not phase him upon this realization. Llewelyn entered the Restricted Area by pulling a discarded access fob from a trash bin earlier. He descended the Staff Elevator toward the basement, and the keyfob granted him access. The elevator doors opened, and he noticed a warning label: 'Death is bad for one's health. Beware of interdimensional hazards.' He made his way down a long corridor with cages lining each side.

Nearly all of the cages, save for one, were illuminated by some recessed lighting. The nearest cage beside him was not. But Llewelyn could feel some type of energy undulating out of it. A spindly arm with claws extended through the darkened bars, startling Llewelyn.

"Have you ever heard the story of Promage the Unwilling?" the Beast asked the nearby cage.

"No, can't say I have," Llewelyn said.

"No matter. Young one, come closer," the Beast spoke as he gestured come hither with its index finger. "I have an enticing wager for you. Care to indulge me?"

"Well... what's the wager?"

"The wager is simple. Answer correctly, and you can walk out alive. Answer incorrectly. The fabric of all realities will collapse slowly," the Beast said.

"No pressure. Okay, let's do it."

He produced the Nixon Half-Dollar from his left breast pocket and placed the coin into one of the Beasts' six hands. It clasped its hand shut, then took its six arms and rapidly twirled each around as fast as possible. It became increasingly difficult for him to track the destination of the coin and its particular hand in the flurry.

"Here, little one. Pick a hand," the Beast said.

He thought for a moment and put the finger on the middle-right hand. The Beast turned that particular palm over and revealed the Nixon Half-Dollar.

"Ha! How about that!"

"I wouldn't be so confident about that, little one."

The Beast turned over the rest of its hands, revealing five more identical Nixon Half-Dollars in each palm. The being cackled with loud laughter and faded out of existence.

Alone. He noticed a calming silence before the recessed lighting flickered in each of the other cells. In the distance, he felt the bass of a low rolling rumble. The sound that followed was sirens, screams, and then nothing.

#

It was not Llewelyn Lowry's first day on the job, but he had been at the San Francisco office for only six months. He had his misgivings about management, but he felt that they were the most consummate professionals. After finishing his ice cream at his desk, two men wearing blue dress shirts, navy slacks, and law enforcement caps stopped beside his cubicle.

"Agent Lowry?" one of them said.

"Yes? What's this about?" Llewelyn said.

"Sir, were you at the Museum of Alternate Worlds yesterday? And did you use the Hall of You?" the other said.

"Yes, I was there, and yes, I did use the Hall."

"We have reason to believe another you may have released the Beast from its captivity in Universe-404."

"Oh shit."

"He may have initiated a level-12 paracosmic collapse."

"Where do you need me?"

"Come this way, sir."

"Of course," Llewelyn said as he rose from his seat and collected his belongings before joining the members of the Bureau of Alternate Affairs' law enforcement arm. The two uniformed men and Llewelyn made their way to the Museum of Alternate Worlds in this universe, located in San Francisco on Pier 19 and not near the rim of the Grand Canyon.

THE RESTAURATEUR

I hired Jimmy soon after Sky quit. I had been hoping to see Sky's back ever since I saw his front. When I hired Sky, he told me that his specialty was à la carte dining as well as catering, yet in the six months that he worked for me he only used the menus of his predecessor, never preparing any à la carte menus of his own. Talented chefs are as common as hens' teeth in northern Vermont — my rationale for not having fired Sky long before. By quitting when he did, however, Sky left a void at an awkward moment as I had committed to cater several important private events in the weeks that followed. I prided myself in quality, service, and keeping our customers happy. A change of chefs in mid-stream can be upsetting. My task was to make the transition as stress free and as inconsequential to my customers as possible, but the truth was, I was glad to be rid of the guy.

Both the catering manager and the owner of the resort in the southern part of the State where Jimmy had previously worked couldn't praise him enough for the quality of his cooking and his work ethic:

'Jimmy's the best. Our customers loved him.'

'Jimmy's food was terrific. Never a complaint.'

'If it were my decision, Jimmy would still be working here.'

'We hated to see him leave. A real team player, that Jimmy.'

Such effusive praise, especially from a former employer and colleague, alerted my suspicions. I recalled Steve, a chef I had hired several years before who was working at a Bed & Breakfast in a neighboring town. Its owners also rained praises of competence and cooperation down on Steve's chef's coat. He spent his first four weeks at my place immersed in trendy chefs' apparel catalogues at the expense of tending to his duties in the kitchen, such as hiring staff to assist him in prepping and during service in the restaurant. Steve possessed none of the qualities he had been praised for. In truth? In this country employers can be sued by former employees if a negative recommendation leads to lack of employment. So why bother asking? I generally didn't, relying on my gut impression on whether to hire someone. When asked for a recommendation, I become as evasive as possible, to avoid potential litigation and to remain honest.

When Jimmy accepted my offer, I was once again thankful that Sky had quit, because my gut was telling me that I now had a winner. Jimmy looked younger than his age, which I would guess to have been in the mid-20s. His beet-red hair, worn messy, complemented his rosy complexion which, I suspected, was enhanced by his too great a liking for liquor rather than Elizabeth Arden products. I knew from my experience, that chefs nursed their weaknesses. I had yet to discover Jimmy's, but booze was a definite candidate.

But we got along, Jimmy and I, seeing eye-to-eye on most aspects of the kitchen. His menus reflected what I, too, believed would be the reason for our customers to return, and he never complained about accepting reservations well past our published closing hour. Within a week, Jimmy had put together the core of a staff that included a motley duo, Tai and Joey, who resembled left-over freaks from a travelling circus. Tai was well over six feet tall, whereas Joey barely reached five feet. Although Tai was in the food-preparation business, he looked anorexic, whereas Joey appeared to have never stopped eating. Both were covered with tattoos from their necks to their short-panted legs.

For dishwashers, Jimmy hired two Russians. They might have been identical twins except one wore his hair parted on the left whereas the other parted his on the right. Apparently, they had a need to support one another at the dish-washer station, making that activity twice as expensive as it ought to have been.

But staffing was part of the chef's responsibilities. I rarely interviewed kitchen staff other than for the chef's position as I knew as much about cooking as they did about operating a restaurant. I assumed that Jimmy had hired qualified people. A red light should have flashed when I saw Tai and Joey, but, as I said, staffing was the chef's domain, along with menus and cooking. My job was to hold things together, not question the hires.

Days turned into weeks. The catering functions as well as à la carte dining seemed effortless. It was the honeymoon phase. Who was I to question or fault an incident or two, unless customers complained or the integrity of the restaurant was imperiled?

One night, perhaps a month into the new season, I dropped by to observe, a habit I was accustomed to do to assure quality. Diana, my floor manager, greeted me with her usual cheerful personality.

"Hi boss."

"Hi, Diana. How's everything?" I asked as I entered from the back door.

"Everything's smooth and beautiful, boss." With these words Diana picked up food from the grill station, to deliver to a table.

Our restaurant had an open kitchen, California-style. No barrier separated the kitchen from the dining area. Customers could eat in front of the cooks while they cooked or grilled or prepared pizzas. It was all part of my keep-it-honest, keep-it-real policy — nothing hidden, including the temperament of the cooks.

Passing the grill station where several customers were eating, I surveyed the dining room. Diana was right. Everything appeared to be calm. People were dining and talking, and the waitstaff were serving. Looking more closely, however, I noticed that every empty table — and there were quite a few — was littered with uncleared, dirty dishes. Not one table had been bused.

My blood pressure must have soared for I saw everything — not just Jimmy's face and hair — deep red, verging on purple. I cornered Diana where no one could see or hear us, as she was returning to the kitchen area, empty-handed.

"Diana, what the fuck is going on?"

"Nothing boss. I'm making you plenty of moola tonight," she replied as she sailed into the grill station for more orders.

"This place is a disaster!" I all but screamed, silently reminding myself that customers were sitting and eating all around us, seemingly oblivious to the chaos.

"Not to worry, boss. I've got everything under control," Diana answered.

"The fuck you do," and with that I decided that my only choice then was to bus tables myself and take care of Diana later.

At the end of the night, I had a chat with Jimmy.

"Jimmy, when I'm not here, you have the responsibility to make sure the place runs smoothly. What happened tonight?"

"I was busy cooking," Jimmy said.

"Okay. You were cooking. But didn't you see the chaos all around you, right in front of you?"

"Yeah, but no one complained. So what?"

Yeah, so what! I realized I wasn't getting anywhere with my relatively new chef, so I let it go. This wasn't a sufficiently important battle.

A few nights later, I asked Diana to come to my office. Over the months there had been too many incidents for me to expect Diana's ways to change: stained linen she used to reset tables; cutlery with egg emblazoned on the fork tines; lipstick smacked on wine glasses into which she poured the water; taking drags from a cigarette she hid in her uniform that caught fire as she was serving the Governor of our State — were just a few of the memorable moments of Diana being my dining room manager.

"Diana, I love you to death, but tonight is your last night. You're fired."

"Paul, I love you too, but can't you give me one more chance?"

"Diana, I've given you perhaps a dozen one-more-chances during the past months. I have no more left in my inventory."

"Paul, I understand. I was just hoping." She hugged me, sucking the breath out of my diaphragm. "I'll always remember you, always."

It wasn't too many days later when David, my bartender who I had promoted to floor manager after firing Diana, informed me that Jimmy had been seen in bars around town at all hours of the day and night.

"Paul, everyone in the business knows ...."

"What David? And who is everyone?" I asked as we sat at the bar of the restaurant, chatting. I liked David; I liked chatting with him. While he had been married — and divorced — four times before turning thirty-five, David was a great bartender — and an attraction for any and all unattached, as well as attached, women who flocked to our bar nightly.

"Jimmy drinks. He's been seen in practically every bar in town, both before and after service in this restaurant," David told me.

This information didn't come as a complete shock. Every time Jimmy approached me, I smelled an overdose of cheap eau-de-cologne. I decided to act. The following day I called Jimmy into my office.

"Jimmy, I know you drink."

"Whad'ya mean I drink?" he bellowed.

"Jimmy, I know you drink. People talk. They see you in the bars and they tell me as well as other employees."

"I never drink on the job," he replied, his voice now less challenging.

"I never said you did. I said that I know you drink. But what's worse is that you try to cover it up with a cheap eau-de-cologne. I'd rather smell booze on your breath than cheap eau-de-cologne emanating from your body. So please, knock off the eau-de-cologne."

And he did. From then on, I smelled whiskey ... or bourbon ... or tequila when around Jimmy, but I never again had to endure the smell of his cheap eau-de-cologne. I couldn't stop his boozing as it didn't seem to hinder his ability to cook.

One Sunday I decided to have dinner at the restaurant, a normal practice of mine, to sample the food as well as the service. I arrived around 7:00, intending to sit at the grill in the kitchen area where I could talk with the cooks. As I entered from the rear entrance, the atmosphere felt ominous. Nothing appeared amiss. It was more like the calm before disaster. I sensed disorder, disarray, derangement in the air. Had Diana returned? As I was sitting on a stool in front of the pizza oven, I looked around.

"Wild night tonight," David said as he handed me a menu.

"Wild, David? Everything looks calm to me."

"Looks, but *look*, Paul. Who do you see?" he replied.

"I see Jimmy. Who else should I see?"

"That's the question," David replied. "You see Jimmy and no one else."

I looked again. I saw Jimmy in front of the sauté station. I saw Jimmy manning the pizza oven. I saw Jimmy making salads. But I didn't see Tai or Joey or Bob, the sous chef. I only saw Jimmy — three or four Jimmys.

"Where is everybody?"

"Gone. All gone."

"What d'you mean, gone?"

"That's what I said, Paul. Gone. Jimmy told them all to leave."

"But how could he?" I managed to blurt out. "We have a full house." The terrace hadn't an empty table and even a few tables in the main restaurant were taken by diners who preferred a/c to fresh Vermont air.

"David, what's happened? Why did Jimmy tell everyone to leave?"

"The guy's fuckin' crazy, that's why," and with this explanation David walked back to the bar to make drinks.

I looked back at Jimmy — all three or four of him — all furiously cooking and plating dinners. Would it have made any difference had I asked him for an explanation then? Other than walking out himself, none. I decided to forgo the discussion until the end of service, forget about eating, and pitch in. We had to get through the night.

Miraculously there were only two complaints that night out of over seventy dinners: one overcooked lamb and one mis-order, and even these customers weren't unhappy.

"The waitress brought me a halibut cheek steak," the mis-order told me. "I'd ordered the rack of lamb, but you know what, Paul? I'm glad your kitchen screwed up, because this halibut is absolutely *fab-u-lous.*"

As I made my way between tables delivering food, I listened, and when I had a moment to spare, I talked to customers. No one criticized the food or the service. No one told me they had waited too long for their food. Everyone was enjoying himself.

"Paul, this *is* the best restaurant in town," a customer from New York told me when I stopped at his table.

"Better than most of the restaurants in the city," his wife corrected him.

"Jamais agneau comme ton chef a grillé le mien," a woman from Paris told me. "Magnifique."

Meanwhile, in the kitchen, Jimmy was flinging food from station to plate, cursing. His face resembling an eggplant. His eyes bulged. His red hair was plastered to his skull. But he appeared to be enjoying the chaos.

During the following week, calm prevailed, with Tai and Joey assisting Jimmy. But on Friday before service David told me that Tai and Joey wouldn't be back.

"Did Jimmy fire them?" I asked, remembering that on the night of Jimmy's one-man performance he had told everyone to go home.

"No," David said. "They're in jail."

"*Jail*? I don't understand. Why are they in jail?"

"Drugs. Tai and Joey are drug dealers," David informed me.

I looked at David, wondering what was going on in my restaurant? I thought I ran a clean place. No happy hour. No free drinks after service. No sexual harassment. No serving drinks to minors. Now my floor manager was telling me we have two drug dealers working the line?

"David, did Jimmy know this when he hired them?"

"What do you think, Paul? He hired them *because* they sold drugs. They were his suppliers!"

Was I naive or just stupid? Where had I been that I couldn't tell the difference between a drug dealer and a line cook? I couldn't let this go, but I also didn't know how to handle David's information.

The following weekend we catered a large wedding brunch at the home of an acquaintance of my business partner. Mike Slater was a Boston lawyer who owned a second home in town. I had handled the arrangements with Mike and his daughter, the bride-to-be. Jimmy's crew set up the barbeque and I supervised. The weather cooperated, a rare experience in northern Vermont, and the guests appeared to be enjoying themselves, complimenting me on both the food and the service.

"Best damn brunch," Mike told me as we were wrapping things up. "I gave Jimmy a couple of "C" bills to spread with his team; hope you don't mind."

At 2 AM my phone rang.

"Paul, this is Mike Slater." Phone calls at 2 AM are never good news.

"Hello, Mike. I hope no one is sick?" Racing through mind was that a guest — or several guests — had come down with food poisoning. Mike was a lawyer. Was he calling to advise me that he was about to sue the restaurant?

"No, no one is sick. But there is a little problem." Mike didn't sound friendly, like when he told me it was the best damn barbecue. "Jewelry and cash were missing from my sister's bedroom where she had left them on her bed and dresser." Relief. I felt like a huge weight had been lifted off of my back. "Since your staff had access to the house during the barbeque, one of them must be a thief." The only staff — other than myself — who had any reason to be in Mike's house were Jimmy and Bob, our sous chef. I could afford to lose Bob, but Jimmy? "What are you going to do about it?"

"Mike, I'm really sorry about what apparently happened during an event that should have been the happiest day for you and your daughter. You have my assurance that I will get to the bottom of this first thing in the morning."

I hung up and tried to sleep. By the time I saw Jimmy that morning I hadn't slept more than a couple of hours, but I had spoken to my business partner, Billy, who Mike had called immediately after he'd called me.

"He asked me what we were going to do about it," Billy told me. "I told him to go fuck himself. We're not responsible for his fuckin' sister's stupidity and negligence. And if he doesn't pay the bill, I'll sue his fuckin' ass. Meanwhile, talk to that fuckhead chef you hired." Billy spoke a distinct fuck patois. He was also one of the best trial lawyers in Montreal.

"I was busy cooking," Jimmy told me. "Speak to Bob; he had been in the house to locate equipment needed for the barbecue."

Later that afternoon, Mike Slater called to tell me that our sous chef had been involved — but never booked — in a half dozen mysterious thefts during the past year.

"My information — if that interests you, Paul — comes from friendly DAs in various cities around New England."

Luckily, I knew that suspicion and indictment were not the same, and while we should have known had the sous chef been indicted because there would have been a police record, we wouldn't necessarily know about his past had there only been suspicions. Some delicate diplomacy would be needed to avoid having Mike Slater spread rumors that we hired thieves, as well as to avoid being sued by an employee for false accusations.

Fate intervened.

Bob disappeared and Billy reminded Mike Slater of an incident in Mike's past that Mike wouldn't want his wife to know about. Mike paid the bill for the barbeque and we never again heard about the theft at his home.

To replace Bob, Jimmy hired Matt who had previously worked for a restaurant in Shelburne. Of Swedish descent, Matt gave me the impression of being honest, friendly, and a person who enjoyed his job.

About a week later — foliage littering the ground, the off-season fast approaching — business was slow. One evening I walked into the restaurant. David, who I asked to take over for me that evening, told me that the couple at table 24 wanted to speak with me.

"Problem?" I asked, cautiously.

"Nothing unusual tonight, Paul," David replied. "Jimmy pulled a knife on Matt. Pinned him to the salad bar counter for five minutes. No blood. Lots of screaming. You know, the usual. Hey, don't forget table 24."

I watched as David walked back to his bar — slowly — to take the orders from customers waiting for him there — a couple of 20-somethings women who, along with quite a few other women, regularly frequented the restaurant to sit at the bar and shoot the breeze with David.

Trying to give myself time to think about how to handle the latest kitchen crisis, I walked over to table 24.

"Hi, Paul. Nice place you have here," the man replied with a soft Southern accent. "Great food. It's the third night the missus and I have eaten here."

"Glad you like it. We try." I was attempting to sound as calm and as friendly as possible. "It's nice to know people like yourselves appreciate what we're doing."

"I hope you don't mind," he said. He looked at his wife and then at me. "But we were wondering ...."

"Yes?"

"We've been here three nights now, and, the food is great, simply the best, but ...."

"Yes?"

"We were wondering ...."

"Yes?"

"We were wondering, what's going on in the kitchen?"

"I'm not sure I understand?"

"Well, the food's great, and David's been wonderful. You've got a beautiful place, but, well, there's a lot of commotion in the kitchen. Screaming. Yelling. We were just wondering ...."

I looked at my two guests at table 24. I didn't know what they had overheard, but I knew that they had heard more than they should have.

"I'll tell you," I said slowly but with a certain freedom that his questioning seemed to have released. "You don't have to go to Iraq to have a weapons-of-mass-destruction experience. All you have to do is eat at The Chelsea Grill and you'll have experienced it all." I stopped and looked at my guests who, with mouths agape, resembled cod fish. "And don't worry about the tab tonight. Your dinners and drinks are on the house." I then bid them goodnight and returned to the bar to talk with David.

"David, I've made a decision. I'm firing Jimmy."

After service I asked Jimmy to meet me in my office.

"Jimmy ...." he looked at me as though I were the enemy he needed to butcher. His eyes were bloodshot, his uniform stained with the remnants of the food he had cooked during his one-man show, and I noticed that his hands were trembling.

"I've been meaning to have this talk with, but your performance tonight ...."

"Yeah, what about it," he uttered, almost sneered. "You have problems with my food?" As he said this, the trembling in his hands became more noticeable. I wondered if he needed something that Tai and Joey supplied him with and hadn't taken it before our meeting.

"It's not about your cooking ...."

"Then what is?" He placed his hands under the table, out of sight.

"It's not the quality of your cooking ...."

"If it's not about my food, and your customers haven't complained, then what exactly is your problem, Paul?" He looked up and into my face, belligerently.

"Okay, I'll come right and tell you. Jimmy, your ways in the kitchen and with the staff you hired ...."

"Yeah, okay, I'm getting the picture ...."

THE RESTAURATEUR

"Allow me to continue," I told him, for now I was becoming not only annoyed but angry. Who the fuck was he to speak to me this way? "Your relationship with the people around you is intolerable ...."

"Yeah, for whom?"

"For me, and I would imagine, for those who work in the same kitchen as you do. Many nights you summarily dismiss all of them and work the line by yourself."

"You have a problem with that?"

"Yes, I do. I opened this restaurant to not only present to our customers the finest food in the region, but also for them to have the most amazing experience anywhere. How do you think they feel when they hear, and see, the chef screaming at his sous chef and threatening him at knife point, while they're trying to enjoy their meal?" I looked at Jimmy, but all I saw was someone who, mentally, wasn't with me. "And this hasn't been the first time this kind of behavior on your part has occurred in my restaurant. You're fired." Jimmy didn't move. I didn't even see him blink. But his mouth began to tremble as though he were about to speak. Silently, he rose and walked out of my life.

When I left my office, I noticed David behind the bar.

"He didn't even say goodbye," David said. "Just left. How about joining me; I think you could use a glass of champagne."

"We both could."

"Now that you're rid of Jimmy, there's something that I've been wanting to tell you." David handed me a glass of champagne. "Close the restaurant."

I looked at him, a little bewildered.

"Paul, you're my friend. You pay me well and I need the job, and as your friend, take my advice and close the restaurant. It's just not worth it. I've worked here for the past two years. I've seen what you've had to put up with. You've had your fun. Quit while you're still enjoying the ride."

We finished the bottle of Veuve Clicquot, gave each other a hug, and left.

That night I closed the restaurant for good. I couldn't remain open knowing that I had an explosive situation in my kitchen. David was right. Twelve years as a restauranteur were enough for me. I thought myself to be an honest businessman, running a reputable operation. How could I tolerate a mad, half-crazed, drug-addicted drunk in my kitchen as my chef and representative, no matter how good his cooking was? I decided: gardening in the summer and making maple syrup in winter were safer pastimes.

About a month later I received a phone call from out-of-state.

"Is this Mr. Howard, Mr. Paul Howard?" the caller asked.

"Yes, this is Mr. Howard."

"My name is Alice Craig. I'm the general manager of the Cooper Hotel in Boston. A former employee of yours, Jimmy O'Connor, has applied for a job with our hotel as Executive Chef, and I would like to ask you a few questions." She paused. "Jimmy O'Connor worked for you until last month. Is that right?"

"Yes."

"As executive chef? And was in charge of catering?"

"Jimmy was our chef, and yes, he was in charge of catering."

"Is there anything we should know about Jimmy?" Alice Craig asked.

Now I was in a quandary. I knew I didn't have to be totally upfront with her, but I had always prided myself on my integrity, on being honest. If I were to tell Alice Craig what I knew, what I had witnessed, and what I suspected, she would never hire Jimmy. I'd been through a situation like this before when I fired an employee who had showed up for service drunk, with an open bottle of tequila that she offered to my manager, and smoking marijuana. When I protested at the unemployment-benefits hearing, I was told by the judge that showing up for work drunk and high on marijuana wasn't a basis for being fired. Therefore, I knew that a half-mad, drug-addicted drunk had more rights in this country than I did. I had to be careful in discussing Jimmy's behavior with Ms. Craig.

"Could you be more specific Ms. Craig?" I replied. "If you're asking if Jimmy is capable ofhandling the job you're offering, my answer would be yes, he is."

"That's not quite what I have in mind, Mr. Howard," Alice Craig answered. "How would you say his relationship was with your other employees?"

Aside from hiring two drug dealers to assure his supply line, of hiring a multiple-suspected thief, and of almost slitting the throat of a cook .... No, I couldn't tell Alice Craig any of that.

"As far as I knew, Jimmy got along with the other staff members," I told her. "There were heated discussions now and then, but as you know, when the restaurant's busy, cooks tend to heat up along with the food. I would say Jimmy's relationship with his staff wasn't unusual." Having just finished reading **Kitchen Confidential**, I knew my answer to be true. In New York, kitchen stabbings, sex, and drug dealing were almost the norm. Jimmy's antics were definitely questionable, if not deplorable, but compared to New York? No, not unusual.

"That's a relief, Mr. Howard. Jimmy appears to be so calm and unexcitable. One more question." I knew, before Alice Craig asked, what she was about to ask me, but I didn't know my answer.

"Mr. Howard, if you could, would you rehire him?"

I knew, and dreaded, that she would ask me that. If I said yes, I would be lying. If I said no, I would be opening my restaurant to a potential lawsuit because Alice Craig wouldn't hire him. I allowed a few minutes to pass.

"Mr. Howard, are you still there?"

"Yes, Ms. Craig. I was merely admiring the scene outside my window. It's a perfectly lovely November day here in Vermont; one of the most beautiful I can remember. But you asked me a question?"

"Yes. I asked if you would rehire Jimmy?"

I stayed in my chair what seemed to be an eternity ... before telling Ms. Craig, "Yes I would."

PYRAMID SCHEME

Sticky, moist, like glue behind his knees. The kind of October warm that used to be called unseasonably warm but by then was called a day like any other. Niko ran his palms against his pants. His first glimpse of the house, upon being dropped off by the morose driver with two cellphones, was of the trellised front yard, the trellises worn and covered in un-manicured vines.

"Look at those stick things with the plants growing all over them. I love those. So old." Porsche joined him with their two bags, which was everything they had except for now the monstrous house in front of them.

"Yeah I love those. It's like a farm." Niko kicked through the leaves, mind-ful of his unblemished sneakers with the white sides and laces. They had cost him one day's pay by the prices of three years ago and two day's pay by the wages of last year. He went to the front door, giddy, reached for the envelope that rested on the nearby windowsill. Inside were keys left by the lawyer; Niko knew by the note inside that contained a lot of letters after the name. He had spoken to the man once on the phone, when Niko was standing outside of the carwash and struggling to hear over the noise of self-service vacuums.

"I have a piece of property I have to give to you."

"Who are you?"

"I'm a lawyer."

"Oh. Okay. So what do you want to give to me?"

"You're Niko, right?"

"Yeah I'm Niko. What do you want to give me? Are you like, a scammer?"

"No I'm a lawyer. There's a woman named Mrs. Avon. Have you ever met her?"

"Don't think so. No. Who is she? I haven't met her."

"Me either. But she's my client. And she wanted to give somebody this house and we found you."

"Give me a house? Who is she?"

"She's just a woman. She had a lot of money and some properties and she was very charitable. Wanted to give things to poor people. Sorry no of-fense."

"That's okay. What kind of lawyer are you?"

"I do this kind of thing. Where are you? It sounds like a spaceship launch.

Like a space shuttle."

"I'm washing my car. Getting it washed. It's a Lexus. Real clean."

"That's nice. Listen I need to give you this house and I need to call a lot of other people so I need to take care of this quickly. Do you have e-mail?"

"What's wrong with my phone?"

"We're old-fashioned."

The details were passed to Niko who didn't want to believe that anything could come to him free. Didn't want to and couldn't believe it because nothing was ever free, least of all a place to live. Now standing in front of the house he could almost believe it.

By the next morning they had passed a night in the house, on top of the same bed that the woman Mrs. Avon had left. Niko planned to get all new things eventually but for the meantime use what was left over. The stuff all seemed perfectly fine to him. He had never had his own house before and didn't know what he was supposed to do exactly, and even though Porsche had never had a house or even a car to drive other people in she had more ideas than he did.

"I think we should get some new curtains. These windows are so bright they let a lot of light in and I don't know if there's a guy we can get out here who can replace all of the windows with ones that you can't see as good into, but if we can't do that then we can get curtains. My mom used to always get new curtains, they cover up a lot of things even if you don't have brand new stuff like windows."

"You mean tinted windows? You want those?"

"Maybe. That might be nice. Nobody could see in. Nobody could see us then, it would just be me and you."

"That's nice."

"I love you, king."

"I love you, queen."

Niko couldn't argue with her desires. But when he looked online and tried to find somebody who could change all the windows, he got overwhelmed because there were about two and a half thousand profiles that came up with guys who were eager to get a job changing out all of the windows in a house even though they had never done it before. Lots of them offering to do it pretty cheap, too, but Niko thought about something that his father had told him once which was that when you actually own something it might cost more to get something done because you have to get it done right. Niko didn't know who to choose and he found it easier to think about something else. The thing about having the house was that there were plenty of other things to think about.

*

Two weeks later the lawyer showed up.

"You're a really tall guy." Niko actually looked up at the lawyer.

"Thanks its been a good thing for me. So this is the house."

"I thought you might have seen it before. Like in a picture."

"No, but it's nice."

"We could have talked over the phone if you don't like meeting people."

"I wanted to meet you. Listen there are some things about this house that you need to be aware of. Things that you agreed to in the contract that you signed."

"Oh. Right."

"I wanted to see it for myself and make sure these things were plausible. If you know what that means."

"Seems possible that I would."

"Mrs. Avon was a sweet woman. You both seem like nice people too. But Mrs. Avon was rich and she got that way through hard work, her and her whole family. She wasn't born rich, she had to grow up first and then work hard for her family to trust her with the money."

"That's great. Wait I thought you never met her?"

"I met her son. He told me about her. She worked hard and she wanted to make sure that same hard work continued. She wanted to give this house to somebody that needed it, somebody who wasn't as well-off as her but who could still work hard. Somebody who might not have a chance in the current market. Not to say they wouldn't in a future market but right now in this market, it didn't seem likely that they could get something of their own. Where's your Lexus?"

"Oh no, that wasn't my car. That was just like the car I drove for work. Driving people around, you know. The company rented me that car but it wasn't mine."

"Yeah that makes sense."

Porsche used two hands and stroked the straight hair that touched the front of her shoulder, the hair that was lighter than her other hair. "How do you know who to give it to then, if you don't know who might not be able to buy a house in the future?" Porsche was genuinely interested in how people gave away their money because it seemed to her to be a completely insane thing to do. She liked to watch TV shows about serial killers and pawn shop owners and luxury real estate agents, people who did things that seemed insane to her.

"We can guess. We're pretty good at guessing who isn't going to be able to buy a house now, and in the future. Educated guesswork I think is how you might say it. Anyway that was you Niko, you were the right guy for her."

"So what do I have to do? Let you come here and throw parties or something? Or like shoot videos?"

"Nothing like that. I mean performance metrics. Do you understand what I mean? Mrs. Avon wanted the house to be productive for a productive person. That person she was hoping would be you. So the house just has to turn into something that makes money. Something that grows. Do you know that's how houses work? It's okay if you don't. I'm here to explain it to you, that's part of what I get paid for. See houses grow value and they grow money for the people inside of them. Mrs. Avon wanted to make sure that would still happen. It's a very productive house, always has been. She didn't want that productivity to go away. Keeping that productivity going, that's also best for you."

"So I have to make this place into a business? Not just live here?"

"Not a business. But it's an asset. And there's land here."

Porsche raised her hand and the lawyer didn't know how to give her permission to speak. "How is the house making money right now? There's no real business or even a small business happening here."

"It makes money when people are living in it. Then it makes more money when it transfers to someone new. That just happened, that's the stage we're in right now. When someone sells a house, the city will reassess the value of the house. So the house is worth a certain amount one day, and the next day it's worth a lot more even though it's the same house but because there are new people in it. Those people are you. And then it can make more money for the next person who is in it, and so on and so on. I'm going to check in on you every year, maybe a few times a year, see how things are going. And make sure that there is value growing here. And collect some of that money to go back into Mrs. Avon's charity."

"So we have to pay you to live here? Like rent?" Niko stiffened up at the thought of paying rent again. He had only stopped paying rent all of two weeks prior but he liked the feeling so much he didn't want to lose it.

"No, but part of having the house is a stipulation that you donate to Mrs. Avon's charity to help people. And that's going to be on top of the property taxes. Those go to the government, those don't go to any real people."

"But the charity stuff does."

"That's right. It goes to her charity, minus my fees."

"Of course. Fees. I get that."

"Look into it. It's all in the paperwork that I sent you."

"We'll have a look. Thank you so much. You're a good lawyer."

A day later Niko and Porsche sat on the back porch looking out at the land behind their new house.

"Niko how much do you think we should give to the charity that the guy was talking about?"

"I don't know. However much he says we should give."

"Yeah but it's a donation so we can choose how much we want to give. Right?"

"I don't think it works like that. I think it's more of a mandatory donation."

"I'm just thinking that we have to do whatever it is that's the right thing to do. I mean it's like we inherited a house, that's the fucking dream you know what I mean?"

"Yeah I know."

"And you know I'm a queen in this world. That means you and the whole rest of the world need to treat me like one. That means treating me like this is my house."

"Yeah you're a queen, but I'm a king. And you have to respect me as a king. It's your house but it's my house. This house is finally giving me what I'm supposed to have, and that's a castle. That's what a king needs."

"A queen needs a castle too."

"Stop with that bullshit. I'm a king. And I love myself."

"Shit. Whatever. I love myself too."

A minute later there was a knock from the front door and Niko got up to answer it, thinking about how cool it was that he was answering the door of his own actual house. Out in front was the delivery guy, with his car still running but him standing at the bottom of the wood steps.

Niko picked up the bag of hamburgers and fries and onion rings. "Thanks man."

"Yeah cool no problem. I never been out to this house."

"Oh no? We just moved here. Maybe you can come back when we order breakfast tomorrow. Thanks man." Niko turned to go back into his house.

"Yeah I've never really even been over to this side of town except since I started delivering fast food."

"Cool you're a local."

"Yeah my whole life. I don't only deliver, I work in town too."

"That's cool."

"What about you what do you do? I mean, just curious. I wanna get me a house like this one day too so maybe if I could figure out what people do to get 'em maybe I could do something like that. That's all."

"Yeah I do a lot of different things, man. Lot of different things. I used to drive too."

"Oh yeah?"

"Yeah. But now not really doing that. Figuring out my next move. Right now this house is kind of what I do, you know? This place is like an investment."

"That's what they say."

"Thanks man." Niko turned again, hungrier than before. But the young kid stopped him.

"You know there was a cemetery around this area. Like, a hundred years ago or something but still it might be true."

"Like right here?"

"All back in these woods. The ones behind your house, the other houses around here. My grandma told me about that. She lived here a long time and she told me that her family is buried back here somewhere. So it's cool to be out here for once."

"That's great for her."

Two days later Niko kicked at a tall rock in the yard, a part of it that was at least a one-minute walk from the rear door. He wore a pair of old sneakers, from the back of his rotation, with black soles and a few scuffs that rendered them worthless. When he crouched down to have a look at the stone he saw marks etched in it, and thought maybe they were even in the shape of letters. He touched one with his fingers, feeling the smooth bore and the cold rock. He pulled his hand back and put his fingers in his jacket pockets, warming them and staying crouched to look from one rock to the next. He couldn't tell what was in a line and what was just laying there with no purpose, marking nothing.

*

A week later Niko walked into town, the whole way cursing his phone service for dying or getting cut off so that he couldn't order a fast food delivery. He walked past a few more big houses, spaced out, until he got to rows of smaller houses that were packed in tight and in straight lines. The smaller the houses got the more straight they got and they really fell in line, and Niko knew that was because the people there were more poor and he was glad that wasn't him anymore. His house had land and he could do whatever he wanted on it.

In the town he found the first store and it was the one that he needed, a mini market with a big sign over the front door and the sign said "mart Mart" in blue letters. Inside was a convenience store with more rows of things laid out in straight lines, neat and orderly. Niko picked at the bags and bottles and carried an armful to the front of the store where the clerk waited.

"You paying card?"

"How much is it?"

"Seven fifty-three."

"Yeah I got a card. Use this one." Niko put out his hand and the clerk took plastic money from him. Niko saw he was an older guy, a grey-haired guy and burly. This guy doesn't take shit, thought Niko. He tried to catch his eye. "I'm new in town here."

"That's nice."

"Yeah, just got a house up the road that way. A big house."

"Congratulations."

"Trying to learn things about here. I thought you had a good name for your store. Like, really clear what it is. It's a 'mart mart.' That's cool."

"When I bought the store it was the Smart Mart but some kids tried to pull the sign off and I didn't fix it. They got the 'S' though."

"Shit. Sorry. So you're the owner though, right?"

"Yes."

"Nice to meet you."

"Yes."

A month later Niko and Porsche walked through their backyard. Porsche stopped him with a hand.

"What was that?"

"I don't know. A bird?"

"Listen."

They listened for sounds in the quiet. Niko looked past trees and through leaves. "I hear it."

"Right?"

Niko saw what she had heard, someone crouched over and scraping dirt. "There's a guy digging." It was a man and at first he made light sounds like the wind, until the grunts got heavier and carried out from deep inside somewhere.

"So let's do something."

"Do what?"

Porsche stepped past Niko. "Hey man stop!" The scraping stopped, the man doing it turned and saw his two observers.

He raised his hands. "Don't kill me. Please."

Niko shook his head. "Drastic, dude. Hey I know you, mart Mart guy."

"You know this piece of shit? How?" Porsche only stared at the man, intimidating him and watching it work.

"When I went to the convenience store. Like, a while ago. He owns the place."

"Oh, right. Sorry mister, owner guy."

The owner got up from the ground, and Niko saw past his feet to where freshly-dug dirt sat in a pile.

"Hey, this is our land."

"Really? I didn't know. I'm sorry."

"What are you doing? Are you digging up our land?"

"No. I'm not. I'm sorry. I didn't know where else to go."

"Yeah but what are you doing? You have to answer a direct question. That's, like, a social norm." Porsche kept staring at him.

"I'm...I was..."

"I already know who you are man so you should just tell us the truth."

"My wife died."

"Okay. Sorry man."

"I didn't know where else to go. I brought her here."

"Wait she's dead and you brought her here? Like, you killed her?"

"No, no. She died. I had to bury her."

"There's places for that. Like, businesses."

"I don't have the money. And this is a cemetery."

"Yeah I heard that but it's not really true. Now it's a house and we live here so it's not really a graveyard anymore, it's actually our land where we live. We own it."

"I thought nobody would notice."

"You thought you could just bury someone and nobody would notice?"

"People used to. I mean it didn't always cost money, people used to do it for free. I thought I could do it for free maybe, like people used to."

"You don't have any money?" Porsche pressed the man, suddenly interested.

"I have some. Just not enough for a funeral. Or a real burial. But I couldn't leave her. I didn't know what to do. I could barely look at her, because I love her too much. Do you know what I mean?"

Porsche looked at Niko and he recognized the cadence of her eyes, her thinking eyes when she had something in mind that she wanted to tell him but couldn't. He waited for her to press forward which she did.

"Whatever a funeral would cost, you could just give us a percentage of that and you could bury her here."

"Really? How much?"

"Like, whatever you have." Porsche got closer to the man. "And we won't tell any cops or anything. Because this shit is like, illegal. Unless we make it our business." Niko looked at the disturbed ground that was filled with a human body, next to the natural ground.

"Okay. Thank you. I don't have much."

"Whatever you have, we can make it work."

Niko jumped in on Porsche's idea. "And if you buy a piece of our land for this, then you own it. Like an investment. When the price of the land goes up and we get more money, you can get some return on your investment."

"Like a percentage?"

"Like a payout. You put money in, you wait, and then you get more money back. That's how it works. So you pay to bury your wife now and then later on it actually pays for itself."

Porsche didn't try to step into Niko's way. She let him work with his words, as she had seen him do before.

"I like the sound of that."

"So if you have a little bit more to put toward the investment now, we can do it that way. You can leave her right here in this spot. And you can get money back later."

"I'd need her to have a special place that I can mark, and come back to."

"Yeah no problem. We'll mark it. How about we go to the house and we can work out the money."

Twenty minutes later the three of them opened small bags of chips in the kitchen and moved money with their phones.

Later that night Porsche climbed into the old bed next to Niko. "We made some money today."

"I know. That was awesome. Like, made some real money too."

"Let's try to make some more money like that."

"You think?"

"I know." Porsche slid on top of Niko and kissed him.

*

Five days later Niko raked sticks along his driveway, pulling them into small plots along the edges of the concrete. A car pulled up and a woman got out and looked back past Niko, at the house.

"Can I help you?"

"You live here?"

"Yes. This is my house."

"Oh sorry I saw you raking."

"Right."

"So you're the homeowner, that's great. I'm Sierra."

"Hi. I'm in the middle of cleaning up the yard. You know?"

"I know what you did for the man at the mart Mart."

"I don't know what you're talking about…"

"I'm not a cop."

"I know that. Believe me, I know that."

"So I'm not a cop, but I know what you did and I think it's great. And I want to know if I can do it too. I have some money."

Ten minutes later Niko and Sierra stood behind the house, in the middle of the trees.

Sierra walked to the base of one tree and looked up at it. She nodded to Niko. "How much would it be here?"

"How much do you have?"

"It's my brother. It's his money, too. He left it to make sure he could have a nice burial."

"Yeah, that's what we can do here."

"But he was really into the stock market. Stuff like that. So I know he would be happy if he saw that I was taking the money and burying him but making some money back on it too."

"That would make anybody happy."

Niko took an envelope filled with cash from Sierra and the next day she came back with her brother's body wrapped in two black sheets and a black trash bag. Niko and Porsche stood a fair distance away while Sierra and some friends and family, all of them dressed in black just like Sierra's brother, cried and held onto each other until it was over. Then everybody got into different cars and left and went on with their lives.

Porsche brought Niko a glass of lemonade. They sat together on the porch to look at their land. "We need to get some more people doing this."

"Yeah. People have money to invest."

"And we have land. To bury people."

"Did you tell anybody else?"

"No, but I can go into town and make sure that people who don't know can know. And then more people will come out here, for sure."

"Especially if they think they can make some money on it."

"Yeah but I just said that. I have to talk to the lawyer. I don't even really know. We should probably buy a couple of TV's or something, make sure we actually spend the money before anyone comes back for it."

Porsche sat up a little straighter, and peered intently at Niko. "Why don't you take some of the money from that woman, Sierra, and give it to the owner of the mart Mart. Tell him that we made some money already. Which we did, by the way. Just tell him that he got some of his investment back. It's called a 'return on investment' and people call that an 'ROI.' I looked that up. But then once you do that for him you know he's gonna tell everybody he knows that there's money to be made out here burying people. That's just good advertising and that shit works. Look, he already told Sierra and that was before an ROI. So now will be even better."

Niko nodded along with her, knowing she was right. "I'm gonna do that."

Niko went down to the mart Mart and by the time he got done telling the owner that there was some money already made, he knew that it was the right thing to be doing.

A week later, there was somebody new out in front of the house and Niko offered him a place to bury his mother. Four days after that somebody else came and they paid for a place to bury their uncle. Niko moved some of the old rocks that were in rows so that they were in new rows. He organized every big stone that he could find so that there were potential markers for people who wanted them. And some people, he saw pretty quickly, came with their own kind of markers. It turned out that people who wanted to bury people, they had their own ideas about what could mark a place. Pretty soon Niko had a bunch of things out on the land in between the trees, things like hats and helmets and old books and baseball bats sticking straight out of the ground.

The guy with the uncle pointed down at the grave site he had just filled in. "Can I come back to see him any time I want? When are you open?"

Niko didn't know what to say so Porsche jumped in for him. "Not anytime you want. We have to keep our own schedule. So how about you come back in a few months, for the first time, after your uncle settles in. That way we can make sure everything is okay for you. And then we can figure out a schedule."

The guy seemed to like the sound of that and left the house.

"How often should we let people come back?"

Porsche shrugged. "Let's worry about getting customers in first. Then we can figure that stuff out. This is a business, the key is getting some momentum and then building on it."

*

A month later the lawyer returned and he found Niko out in front of the house stringing a wire-mesh fence between wooden posts that he had already driven into the ground. The lawyer looked down at his phone in his hand and called out to Niko. "Hey there. How's it going?"

Niko reached down and brushed away some dirt from the top of his yellow shoes. Yellow shoes with purple soles, and the yellow had a proclivity for collecting and showing dirt. Niko wished he had time to change his shoes for the lawyer but he didn't. Instead, he gathered up his usual confidence to share. "Been waiting for you, believe it or not."

"I don't believe it. Really?"

"Yeah really. Can't you take a joke, man? I'm just saying I made some money on the house. You were right."

The lawyer looked up from his phone. "You made money? How much?"

"Enough for a donation." Niko walked up the steps into the house and returned a moment later with an envelope of cash. He gave it to the lawyer, who looked past him to the house.

"Place looks good. You made money? What did you do?"

"Just started running a business. Like we said we would. We just needed the space to do it, you know. What, you didn't believe in us?"

"Not that at all. It just happened fast. That's good for you."

"Is that enough? For now, I mean."

"Yeah, it's enough for a donation, plus fees. Place looks good."

"You already said that."

"It does. What's the fence for? There's nobody around. That's one of the nice parts of living in your own house, you know."

"Just in case. There are deer and stuff out here too. Figured I could put a fence around the place. So when you coming back again?'

"Not sure. I can let you know. Keep up the good work."

Niko waved at the lawyer in his car as he drove away, standing like a homeowner at the end of his street in front of his house doing as he pleased.

*

Three weeks later, Niko had helped thirteen more people bury people on his land. The stones that had once stood in a row were strewn about, as Niko and Porsche had allowed people to choose anywhere they wanted, within reason, to dig their own graves.

"This is one of those things that people always say you have to pay someone else to do it for you, but in reality people have always done this. Like, in ancient times there was no industry for this." One of Niko's customers was exuberant over the idea of saving money and making money and doing things in a traditional way.

"There is a lot of stuff like that. Like food, people used to make their own food."

"Yeah and everybody dies so it's crazy that it becomes this business, you know? Like, literally everybody has to die but people figured out how they could make a ton of money on that."

"It's crazy. I know. But it's good business though."

"Now, we can make money on it. We can make money on our own friends and family dying. That's really kind of original human, in a way. Like, we're taking ownership over this very human thing that happens to all of us and I think that's beautiful. Like, that's queen shit."

Everywhere Niko looked the ground was disturbed, either recently or within the last few months. There was no more grass, it was all churned by metal and bones. The piles of leaves, where there were any that hadn't been swept away by the wind, were in-between the lines that separated one grave from the next.

Niko and Porsche went to work on the little plots, smoothing them over and spreading grass seed where they could.

"Do you think this can grow quick?"

"It says on the package that it will." Porsche handed Niko the package for him to look for himself.

"It needs to grow quick because we don't have any more land and people are gonna see that if they come back here looking for a place."

"There's a car pulling up right now."

"Shit, what can we do if we don't have any more land for them? Like, right now what can we do?"

"I'll go talk to them. You keep planting." Porsche went around to the front of the house, her house, and waved at someone who was getting out of their car. Before they could pull the large bundle from their trunk, Porsche talked to them to stop them.

Niko could hear her far in the distance. But he stopped listening when he saw the foot sticking out of the ground nearby. Not a foot with a shoe on it, not even an old shoe that wasn't worth anything, but a naked foot with painted toenails. Niko shuddered, and closed his eyes and dug with his shovel to scoop dirt and toss it toward the foot. When he had tossed enough he opened his eyes and looked and didn't see the foot anymore. He sat down, exhausted, and Porsche came back to him.

"What's wrong?"

"There must have been a storm or something. Or an animal. There was a foot sticking out of the ground."

"Shit. That's gross. I told that lady to come back tomorrow."

"What can we do before then?"

"We have to do something. People are ready to pay."

"What if… no."

"You have an idea? You have to tell me."

"What if we got rid of some of these customers. Just got rid of them and put new people in there."

"Yeah. Like, replaced their spot with someone else."

"Yeah. Like they're just renting the land anyway, investing in it. We could leave part of them. But we could get rid of most of them."

"We could burn them. And even leave some of the ashes."

"Yeah. And then people could come visit still. And if they have a marker, we just have to write down where it was and who it was. It's like consolidation."

"Yes! Okay. And then when people come visit we just put the marker out. They don't actually look at the body anyway. That's how a cemetery works."

"Yes. Yes. That's it. Okay. We just have to dig up some of these bodies."

"I love you, king."

"I love you too, queen."

Niko set to work with the shovel and Porsche set to work with her phone, taking pictures of all the places on the land that had bodies. She wrote down whatever names she could remember or find and put them all on a list in her phone, to be accessed anytime.

*

Two hours later, even through the handkerchief wrapped around his face, Niko found it difficult to breathe without gagging. The first legs and arms that he had pulled out of the ground, they came off like he was breaking apart tender chicken wings and he closed his eyes and flung them away to start a new pile. The stench of the bodies got to him and got inside his throat and he worried he might never get it out.

He took a stick and held his lighter to it until it burned a cherry ember at the end. But when he held it to the closest toe pointing at him, what he expected to happen didn't happen.

Niko went to the house, exhausted and struggling to forget what the stench of human flesh tasted like. He found Porsche on the back stoop. "They aren't burning."

"Did you try lighting the clothes?"

"Yeah I tried that."

"We need gas. That's what we need."

"Oh, like lighter fluid for a barbecue. Yeah, you're right."

PYRAMID SCHEME

Sheepish, Niko trudged down to the mart Mart and avoided eye contact while he bought every can of lighter fluid that was in the store. The owner didn't pay him too much attention anyway, and Niko stole a peek to see and found that the owner stared past him to the back drink coolers. Head still down, Niko got out of the store and carried the plastic bag of fluid back up to the house.

With enough squirts and dousing, the foot went up in flames. Niko watched it burn for a moment to make sure it was burning and then he ran away from the fire, the smell and the smoke. When he got back to the stoop of the house, he sat next to Porsche and they watched the black plume rise between the tallest trees, growing even taller than any of them.

"That worked."

"Yeah, looks like it."

*

A day later a man showed up with a truckload of bricks in the bed of his pickup truck. He surveyed some of the land, dotted with piles of black ash. Porsche greeted him, glancing back at Niko far behind her in the woods, his face covered in black soot. "Can we help you?"

"I want to build a mausoleum."

"Like a tomb?"

"Like a little pyramid. I'm a bricklayer. I can do it."

Porsche didn't bother asking Niko for his particular opinion, she knew that he agreed with her in principle. "Okay. How much do you have?"

"Don't you tell me how much it costs and then I decide?"

"This isn't that kind of business."

The bricklayer told her how much he had and she asked for most of it. He got to work right away.

Two weeks later, a pyramid of bricks stood in the middle of the yard, on top of and surrounded by stones and markers. Niko and Porsche had moved what they were able to move, and cataloged it too. What they didn't have time to rebury, they burned and made a note of it. They felt confident that they had everything accounted for on their phones.

Niko offered a can of soda to the bricklayer, who took it and drank it while he looked up at the top of the pyramid, the uppermost bricks. Niko looked past him to the opening in the side. "So that's the door?"

"Yeah, you just pull that big board out of the top up there, and when you do then a bunch of bricks are going to slide down and cover up the door. Like a landslide. That's how the Egyptians did it too."

"That's awesome. So who's this for?"

"It's for me."

"I mean who in your family."

"No it's for me. Actually for me."

"Oh. That's thoughtful of you."

A few days later the bricklayer's wife brought his body in his truck and Niko and Porsche watched her and some guys pull his body into the pyramid. They yanked out the board and the bricks fell and that was that, they went away.

"He made a good investment." Porsche walked around the base of the pyramid, inspecting it casually.

"He bought a lot of land."

"So his family will get a lot of money when the price goes up. That was nice of him."

"Very thoughtful. Might have been the best thing he could have done for them. Buy the land, I mean. Or, rent the land."

"And now we have a pyramid here which could be really useful. I saw inside of it yesterday, there's definitely room in there for more than just one guy. I'm just saying."

A week later a woman came back to see her buried husband. Niko checked with Porsche and they saw that they had moved his ashes after burning him, but they still had a record of the original place. While Porsche stalled a few minutes and offered the woman a lemonade, Niko hustled around to the back of the land and put a marker down just like it had been before. The woman went and talked to the idea of her dead husband while Niko and Porsche watched from a distance.

The next day another customer returned and asked to see their grandmother's grave. Niko obliged, walking them in circles for as long as he could while he figured out where it was. Two days later, a customer came back and didn't want to see anyone at all, they only wanted to ask about the return on their investment.

"It has been a lot of months. There must be some money by now."

"These things can take years. ROI isn't always fast."

"Yeah but you agreed in a contract and I have it in writing."

"Oh, right. Yeah, there's some money. Not a lot but there is some. Let me get you some." Niko went into one of the envelopes that had been left there by a recent customer and he fished out a stack of money. "This should be enough for now. How much is in your contract?"

"That looks right."

"Okay, good. Do you want to see your brother's grave?"

"No, I can come back another day."

"Okay but next time it's just the grave, not the money. Okay?"

During the next weeks, people came back to visit every day. Niko worked constantly, hardly sleeping, to move bodies and burn bodies and dig new holes and scatter ashes. He dumped piles of dirt on piles of soot and stacked rocks on top of that. He pushed around markers and he lined things up so that they were in a row one day, and out of whack the next day.

Every customer that came back, Porsche would check her phone first and see what they were expecting and then Niko would make it happen.

"This is really tiring. I'm like, working every single day. All day. This isn't supposed to be how an investment works. We're not supposed to have to work."

"Yeah but people are still bringing in money so we have to do it. You're a king, you got this."

"I'm a king but you're my queen and right now there's nothing royal going on here. I'm working my ass off right now. That's not king shit."

"A little bit longer."

"What longer? We don't have any land left now. There's no more land."

"That's not true. We have land."

"Where? I went under the house already. In the basement. You know that's full now, right?"

"I smelled something funny, didn't know that's what it was…"

"That's what it was. The basement and the front yard. The backyard, I've dug up everything twice. Every tree, every root is touching something or some-one. There's no more room, Porsche. Even when I burn them, there's ash left. I have to burn everyone. I don't even know if I can do that."

"Yeah but people are still paying." Even as she said it, a car pulled up to the house, paused for a moment, and then pulled away.

"The pyramid already has five people in it. And every time their relatives come I have to change how the bricks look. The other day I even had one family on one side of the pyramid and one family on the other side of the pyramid. At the same time. Like, they didn't know that the other one was there talking to their own dead guy. Because I have five husbands in there. What if all five wives or families come back at one time? There's only four sides to the pyramid. I mean, any pyramid only has four sides, right?"

"I think there's actually still room in there Niko."

"There isn't. There isn't. Oh great look at this shit." Niko pointed out the window. A new car had pulled up, and out stepped the lawyer.

Niko and Porsche went outside to greet him but they weren't able to say anything, only stand in front of him and look glum and tired.

"You guys don't look so great. What's going on?"

"This house is a lot of work."

"Right. You have some money, though?"

"How much?"

"How much do you have?" The lawyer checked his phone and looked up at them, expecting.

"We have some. I'll get some. You were just here, weren't you?"

"That was months ago. I told you I'd be here every few months. The time flies when you own a house. Are you sure you have the money? How's the business?"

"Busier than ever."

"Yeah, same for my business. People need lawyers more than ever. Which is good for me and other lawyers. My friends, you know."

Niko handed him some money.

Porsche sat down on the porch and hung her head. She thought of everything that Niko had told her and how little land was left, the land that had been theirs but that was now filled with the bodies of people who weren't all that different from them. She wondered where she had gone wrong, how she hadn't figured out how to run a business perfectly on her first try. It was supposed to be possible, for anyone even people like her and Niko, people who were smart even if other people didn't always know it.

Niko glanced at her but focused back on the lawyer. "How much is the house worth now? If we sell it?"

"You want to sell it? That's not a good idea."

"You said it goes up in value, right? So what if we sell it? What's it worth?"

"Do you owe somebody money? Is that why you need to sell it?"

PYRAMID SCHEME

Niko ran over in his mind the square footage of bodies, the amount of people who had rented land from him and the amount of return on investment they were expecting. They were big numbers to think about. "Some, yeah. Not a lot but yeah, a little bit. It might just be better to get out now, do another business."

"You can't sell it yet. Okay? You can't."

"But it's our house—"

"It was a gift. You don't sell that. You make use of it. Jesus Christ. You can't sell a house you just moved into. That's not how it works. I know you don't know about these things but trust me, that's not how it works."

"But there's ROI. We know about that." Porsche ran her hands through her hair, feeling frantic.

Niko turned to her to calm her, but stayed engaged with the lawyer. "So, we can't sell it? You won't help us?"

"I didn't say that. Let me think about it. You just shocked me asking about that. Selling the house. Let me think about it. I'll call you tomorrow, okay?"

*

The next day the lawyer didn't call. The day after that, he still didn't call. The day after that, Niko looked out the window and saw a line of cars down the street. The leaves were starting to turn, it was fall again. He knew it had been over a year since the house had fallen on him, the greatest thing that had ever happened to him. He nudged Porsche awake and they looked out the window together.

"Who are they?"

"Customers. I guess they want some money back."

"Yeah. I guess."

Niko walked out to the backyard with her. From somewhere out front, a car horn honked. And then another. There were shouts from people and Niko heard the chicken wire rattle and then the wooden fence rattle. He walked Porsche away from the house, toward the back of the land. At the distant edge, where people had so often brought vehicles with bodies, there were more cars and more people waiting for them.

"What do you wanna do?"

"There's still a little bit of room. Come on." Niko walked her to the pyramid and he pulled two bricks off, one with each hand, and tossed them up to the top where a piece of wood stayed wedged. Porsche followed his lead and soon there was a hole big enough for both of them to fit into.

"Let me go before you."

"Okay, queen. I love you."

"I love you too, king."

Porsche went inside the pyramid and Niko followed her. The smell didn't bother him too much. The voices from outside of the pyramid faded, became more faint, and it was dark inside. He reached outside and up to where the board was, and when he pulled on it an avalanche of bricks came down and cut off the last of the light.

Niko couldn't hear, and neither could Porsche, because they were buried under bricks, the sound of the people scampering through the woods and turning over stones, and the house being ripped down board for board, and the wails and cries of those who had lost everything, and from somewhere under a pile of sticks or leaves or maybe even bones, the sound of his phone going off when the lawyer called.

BIOGRAPHIES

B.A. O'CONNELL spends their time reading poetry and watching bad horror films. They are also quite found of listening to vinyl while making art—-they live in Nowhere, Texas and are currently working on their MFA at Lindenwood University. They have two beautiful cats.

MATTHEW FREEMAN is the author of seven books of poems, most recently *I Think I'd Rather Roar.* He holds an MFA from the University of Missouri-St Louis. Much of his work documents his struggles with schizophrenia.

MAUREEN MARTINEZ (she/her) is an emerging poet who has been working as a counselor at an all-boys Catholic high school in New York City for over 20 years. She has four grown sons. Even the dogs are male. She comes from a long line of Irish ramblers, barefoot dancers and raucous storytellers, which explains a lot. When not reading or writing on the porch, she is trail running or dreaming about mountains. Her poetry is published by or forthcoming in *Meniscus, Folly Journal, She/He Speaks 2, Washington Square Review, The Listening Eye* and *Gramercy Review.*

JONATHAN CHIBUIKE UKAH is a Pushcart Prize-nominated poet from the UK. His poems have been featured in the *Atticus Review, San Antonio Review, The Ephemeral Literary Review, Strange Horizons, The Pierian, The Unleash Lit* and elsewhere. He is the winner of the Alexander Pope Poetry Award 2023 and the second runner-up of the Wingless Dreamer Publishing Poetry Prize 2023.

JULIA LUDEWIG is a learner, teacher, and traveler who splits her time between the U.S. and Germany. She teaches German and Environmental Humanities at a small liberal-arts college in Pennsylvania. In both her academic and poetic worlds, writing is her preferred mode of thinking through the things that matter.

LEWIS LEICHER has returned to Poetry, now that he has retired, after an almost 40-year break (for which Poetry has not yet forgiven him). During that break, he worked as an attorney, including for almost 20 years for WebMD. He has lived in San Diego since 2001 and, before that, lived in and around New York City for most of his life.

STEPHEN BARILE is an award-winning poet from Fresno, California, and Pushcart Prize nominee. He attended public schools, Fresno City College, Fresno Pacific University, and California State University, Fresno. His poems have been anthologized, published in numerous journals, both print and on-line. He taught writing at Madera College, and CSU Fresno.

GERARD SARNAT MD's won San Francisco Poetry's 2020 Contest, Poetry in Arts First Place Award/Dorfman Prizes; nominated for handfuls of 2021/previous Pushcarts/Best of Net Awards; authored *HOMELESS CHRONICLES, Disputes, 17s, Melting Ice King.* He's widely published including by academic-related journals Stanford, Oberlin, Wesleyan, Johns Hopkins, Harvard, Pomona, Brown, Penn, Dartmouth, Columbia, University Chicago; *Ulster, Gargoyle, MainStreet-Rag, Northampton Review, New Haven Poetry Institute, American Journal Poetry, Vonnegut Journal, 2020 International-Human-Rights-Art-Festival, Poetry Quarterly, New Delta Review, Buddhist Review, Brooklyn Review, LA Review, Monterey Poetry Review, San Francisco Magazine, New York Times.* Mount Analogue selected KADDISH for distribution nationwide Inauguration Day.

STEPHEN GRANT is a retired lawyer, poet, and writer, (co-author of 149 Paintings You Really Need to See in North America). He lives in Toronto with his spouse and Maine Coon cat, Felix.

STARRY KRUEGER is a San Diego based writer, teacher and director. She is the founder of Imaginary Theater Company, a theater company committed to producing original plays that empower children to be the heroes of their own stories. Her plays *Dream Train, Mama Threw Me So High, He Who Speaks* and *Canary Cockroach Phoenix* have been published by Drama Notebook. *Dream Train* recently celebrated its first international production in Morocco. Starry is a proud member of the Dramatist's Guild and TYA/USA. (Instagram: @imaginarytheaterco)

NATASHA N. DEONARAIN is the author of two chapbooks, *50 études for piano* (Assure Press Publishing) and *urban disorders* (Finishing Line Press). She's the winner of the 2020 Three Sisters Award by *NELLE* magazine and Best of the Net Nominee by *Rogue Agent Journal.* Recent work has been published in *Third Wednesday* and *Coffin Bell.* She was born in South Africa, grew up in Canada and now lives in Arizona.

BIOGRAPHIES

BENJAMIN FRANDSEN is a writer, journalist, and graphic novelist whose published work spans fiction, poetry, and screenwriting. He was announced as the writer for an upcoming graphic novel series with Immortal Studios at 2023 San Diego Comic-Con. His work has been published by *The Davis Vanguard, Prison Journalism Project,* the Vera Institute of Justice, *UCLA Magazine,* and Columbia University's *exCHANGE magazine.* A PEN America award-winning writer, he has contributed to multiple PEN anthologies and was a finalist for the Writing for Justice Fellowship. His memoir excerpt *Some Mother's Darling* was published by the Vera Institute of Justice. He holds an English degree from UCLA, where he graduated with honors, and is now studying for an MFA at SDSU.

ROSHAN MOAZED graduated from Brown University with a degree in Creative Writing in 2017, and later went on to obtain a degree in Applied Mathematics from UMass Boston, as well. They see math and writing as actually being quite similar; both involving large amounts of creativity, puzzle solving, and thinking outside the box. They work as a data analyst at an environmental investment firm in New Hampshire, and in their free time they can be found writing prose poetry, making jewelry, coding AI chatbots, watching Seinfeld, and chasing the sunset. They are also in the process of writing a short novel, and have fourteen poetry publications to date.

ERICA HOFFMEISTER is an educator, scholar, and multi-genre writer, and is the author of three hybrid/poetry collections: *Lived in Bars* (Stubborn Mule Press, 2019), *Roots Grew Wild* (Kingdoms in the Wild Press, 2019), and *All the Parts You Haven't Lost* (ELJ Editions, 2024). She is also the co-editor-in-chief of the upcoming collection *Take the Fruit: An Anthology of Religious Trauma* (Listen to Your Skin Press, 2024). Originally from southern California, she's she now lives in Denver where she teaches writing.

PHILLIP A. LEAVENWORTH is a former Los Angeles Times employee with a deep affinity for quality science fiction, fantasy, and horror. He received his BA in English Rhetoric and Composition from CSU Long Beach in 2023. He has three Associate's degrees: English, Journalism, and Creative Writing from Long Beach City College, with designs on at least one more. He has participated in Long Beach City College's Creative Writing program since 2011. He is an MFA in Creative Writing student at San Diego State University and intends to explore a doctorate someday. He now lives in San Diego with his fiancée.

E.P. LANDE, born in Montreal, has lived in the south of France and now, with his partner, in Vermont, writing and caring for more than 100 animals. Previously, as a Vice-Dean, he taught at l'Université d'Ottawa, and he has owned and managed country inns and free-standing restaurants. Since submitting less than three years ago, more than 100 his stories — many auto-fiction — and poems have found homes in publications on all continents except Antarctica. His story "Expecting" has been nominated for Best of the Net. His debut novel, "Aaron's Odyssey", a gay-romantic-psychological thriller, is to be published in 2025.

C.M. VINCENT is a writer from San Diego. In his fiction he asks about the culture of capitalism, perceptions of California, and the ways people handle obligations they are born into.

EDWARD MICHAEL SUPRANOWICZ is the grandson of Irish and Russian/Ukrainian immigrants. He grew up on a small farm in Appalachia. He has a graduate background in painting and printmaking. Some of his artwork has recently or will soon appear in *Fish Food, Streetlight, Another Chicago Magazine, The Door Is A Jar, The Phoenix,* and *The Harvard Advocate.* Edward is also a published poet who has been nominated for the Pushcart Prize multiple times.

ASHLEY KAPLAN is a San Diego based photographer who specializes in working to empower the subjects she works with. She has been working as a photographer for eight years, and full time for two years. Ashley enjoys all things photography and the majority of the time you will find her with a camera in hand. If you catch her on the occasional moment without a camera in tow, you might find her running, hiking, painting, and hanging out with friends. To find more of Ashley's work, please find her on Instagram @kaplan.photographyy